Doubles

The Enigma of the Second Self

RODNEY DAVIES

ROBERT HALE · LONDON

© *Rodney Davies 1998*
First published in Great Britain 1998

ISBN 0 7090 6118 8

Robert Hale Limited
Clerkenwell House
Clerkenwell Green
London EC1R 0HT

2 4 6 8 10 9 7 5 3 1

Photoset in North Wales by
Derek Doyle & Associates, Mold, Flintshire
Printed in Great Britain by
St Edmundsbury Press Limited, Bury St Edmunds
and bound by
WBC Book Manufacturers Limited, Bridgend

Contents

Acknowledgements

My heartfelt thanks go to the British Library, where much of my research for this book was done, and to those individuals who assisted me either by bringing their own double experiences to my attention or by helping me flesh out the details of others. The former are mentioned in the text, the latter include Dieter Pevsner of the Schubert Society, Gilbert Davis, Elma Dangerfield of the Byron Society, Christine Kenyon-Jones, Virginia Murray of John Murray Ltd, Peter Underwood of the Ghost Club Society, Somerset Studies Librarian David Bromich, John Selch of the Indiana State Library, and Jennifer Wigley of the Indiana State Archives. Special thanks go to my aunt, Peggy Sullivan, who despite ill-health sent me two interesting Sussex cases in addition to the one involving herself.

The copyright material shown below is kindly reprinted by permission of the publishers.
Celia Green and Charles McCreery, *Apparitions*, Hamish Hamilton, 1975; Helen Creighton, *Bluenose Ghosts*, McGraw-Hill Ryerson Ltd, 1956; Wellesley Tudor Pole, *The Silent Road*, Neville Spearman Publishers, imprint of the C.W. Daniel Company Ltd, 1972; Joan Forman, *The Mask of Time*, MacDonald and Jane's, 1978; *Eirik the Red and other Icelandic Sagas*, trans. Gwyn Jones, The World's Classics, Oxford University Press, 1961; Charles Seltman, *Wine in the*

Ancient World, Routledge & Kegan Paul Ltd, 1957; Peter Ackroyd, *My Interpretation of Dreams: A Time Machine, The Times*, 1996, Sheil Land Associates Ltd; Fay Weldon, *How I was Cured of Nightmares, The Times*, 1997, Curtis Brown.

Illustrations

Line drawings are by Rodney Davies

Introduction

Many years ago, long before I knew anything about the subject of this book, namely the double or *doppelgänger*, I became very interested in what was then called astral projection. This happens when, or so I understood from my reading about the subject, the spiritual or astral body separates itself from the physical body, wherein it normally resides, thus enabling it to visit, often with great rapidity or even instantly, another location, which may be very many miles away.

The separated astral body, which has, according to most commentators, a variable shape, carries with it the consciousness of the person concerned, and is thereby aware of its new surroundings, although quite how it perceives them, bereft as it is of eyes, ears or other sense organs, was left unexplained. However, this apparent sensory lack is partly, or even wholly, offset, I gathered, by the heightened paranormal abilities of the separated consciousness, which allows it not only to view its surroundings but also to read the thoughts of those it meets. It is, moreover, completely invisible to anyone else, and being non-physical it has the curious property of being able to pass without hindrance through walls, doors and other solid barriers, much like the traditional ghost, which gives it access to anywhere. Hence it is a vehicle, apparently possessed by us all, that has supernormal and barely believable powers and capabilities, from which nothing is secret and no one is secure.

Introduction

Most people who experience astral projection, nowadays known as an out-of-body experience or OBE, do so spontaneously, when the conditions are somehow right for it to happen, which unfortunately usually only takes place once in a lifetime. Yet it can also be induced, and because I was too impatient to wait for it to happen on its own, so to speak, I decided to try and bring it about.

The literature about astral projection mentions a number of ways in which this can be achieved, yet all require a great deal of mental effort, as self-induced astral projection is essentially the triumph of mind over matter. What you have to do, to put it at its simplest, is to lie on your bed and will your astral self to be where you want it to be. The technique is helped by you visualizing your destination or the person whom you wish to visit, or alternatively by imagining that you are leaving your body through an aperture in your cranium, located above the third eye, rather like smoke from a chimney. If you are happy to project into your own home, desire and concentration can be fostered by drinking a glass of salt water before lying down, as the intense thirst this causes will help externalize your astral body and direct it to a glass of water left in another room. Or alternatively, you can intone 'Out of my body, out of my body' over and over again like a mantra.

I tried all of these methods but without success. Indeed, I remained lying on my bed like a log, frustrated and disappointed. It seemed that either I had insufficient concentration to perform a Houdini-like escape from my own body or that those who had written about the phenomenon were simply telling an untruth, presenting a fiction as fact.

And had I not discovered, quite by accident, a technique that worked for me, I might have given up. But fortunately, I had earlier begun to practise what is known as contemplation, which is the complete stilling of the mind to hopefully attain union with God or enlightenment. This was the complete opposite of what I supposedly had to do to bring about astral projection, yet I soon noticed that mental quietude brought about some interesting inner events which suggested the stirring of something within.

It is, however, extremely difficult to stop thinking, and when one does it lying down, as I was, falling asleep, rather than union with God, tends to happen. Buddhist monks and other Orientals meditate by sitting cross-legged, with straight backs, but this unnatural posture can only be adopted with difficulty and some discomfort by the untrained Westerner, which hardly assists in calming the mind. Lounging in a comfortable chair with one's head supported is perhaps an acceptable alternative, although I persisted with lying on my back, with my head raised up somewhat on one or two pillows. The tendency to drop off, I found, could be lessened by avoiding doing one's contemplation when tired, and by catching oneself when a tumble into the realm of Somnus was about to occur.

The mind, like nature, abhors a vacuum, which seemingly accounts for its compulsive urge to fill itself with thought, no matter how trivial, unnecessary, repetitive or pointless this might be. It would rather worry about the dog's dinner than take a break, although few of us realize quite how much like a drug addict, seemingly desperate for its fix of thought, the mind is, until we actually make a conscious effort to shut it down. Try it some time: if you can manage ten completely thoughtless seconds you will have done well. You will in fact find that thoughts constantly come into being, demanding your attention like petulant children, and that as fast as you batten the hatches down on one, another, just as insistent, will spring up to take its place. Insomnia sufferers will know what I'm talking about: your minds hate letting you get any rest.

But progress can be made with the right approach. Any attempt to achieve mental stillness should obviously not be made when you have a genuine worry, as this is asking too much, or when your surroundings are noisy or in any way disturbed. Quietness without is necessary to achieve quietness within. Familiar surroundings, such as those of your bedroom, are likewise conducive to your end, and you must also be warm, in good health, and comfortably dressed. Clearly, you can't chase away thought when you are feeling cold, or are suffering from some physical indisposition or pain, or are wearing corsets or tight jeans. Darkness or near darkness is similarly beneficial to contemplation, as any light entering your eyelids tends to prompt cerebration. A contented stomach is also helpful, but avoid a bloated one: intestinal rumblings can be as distracting as a neighbour's amplifier reverberating through the floor or ceiling, and unfortunately flatulence never wafted anyone into oneness with God.

Once I had brought my thoughts under some control, to the extent that I was able to enjoy short periods when my mind was a dark void, I noticed that I developed a tingling in my hands and, although to a lesser extent, in my feet. More remarkably, I also often felt what seemed like a cool breeze blowing over my face, which was frequently followed by, or accompanied by, a noise resembling a high-pitched whine in my ears, yet this was not loud or in any way unpleasant. These essentially physical accompaniments were not only rewarding in themselves, but they seemingly promised further developments and thus encouraged me to keep at it. And with practice and persistence I took ever more control of my mind, which eventually fulfilled its promise, although in a completely unexpected way.

When one's thoughts are stopped and the mind becomes a silent emptiness, it doesn't stay that way for long, because the cessation of thought enables different mental images to come, or manifest, into consciousness. Early on I remember seeing a giant eye form in the blackness within my mind, through whose pupil I seemingly floated, to find myself in yet another blackness, while on a later occasion I witnessed a procession of robed figures, some old and bearded, others young and beardless, troop one by one out of the same darkness to stare at 'me' with a curious gaze, as if wanting to know what I was up to. And more than once I saw strange interlocking geometrical figures, similar to those produced by magic mushrooms, which were quite stunning in their complexity and beauty.

However, while these shapes and scenes were intensely interesting, they were soon followed by two dramatic developments that brought me to the realization that the mental quietness I had been encouraging was a key, if not the key, to separating my consciousness completely from my physical body.

The first of these, I found, happened when my mind was kept thoughtless for some little while, usually twenty minutes or longer, when it quite suddenly and unexpectedly underwent what can only be described as a brisk enlargement, one accompanied by an audible click or start, so that its volume seemingly became greater than that of my cranium. This also brought on a whining noise or a humming in my ears, if one or the other of these had not already occurred, and it was usually partnered by a gentle swaying of the enlarged consciousness from side to side. Together, these changes gave an immediate sense that my mind had somehow jumped into another state.

I soon discovered that the swaying of my mind, which in effect causes a loosening of the bonds of consciousness, is the first, yet perhaps the most important, step of the process that eventually leads to the projection or separation of the astral body, and thereby, in my case, of 'me' from 'myself'. However, it also made me quite anxious, as I did not know what would follow or where I might end up, and at first such fears prevented me from staying in the mind-expanded state.

But later on curiosity triumphed over trepidation, and I found that by holding myself in the state of expanded consciousness I reached the next stage, when the rest of my inner self was apparently freed from its bonds within the physical body. This likewise happened suddenly and unexpectedly, and resulted in a quite violent shaking and shuddering within my whole body, somewhat similar to that caused by a bout of flu, yet different in that it was not a vibration affecting my muscles or skin, but was instead confined to something internal, something that until then I did not know existed.

This shaking and shuddering, like that which affects the body of an aircraft when the engines are revved up, brought with it the overwhelming sense that I was about to go somewhere, yet whether from alarm or instinctive resistance, or from simply starting to think again, the first two or three times I reached this apparent take-off point nothing further happened. The engines ran down, so to speak, and I returned to ordinary consciousness; then I went to sleep.

The journey beyond happened the next time I stayed the night with my girlfriend, whose presence gave me the extra confidence and determination I needed. After we had gone to bed and had made love, when she went to sleep, I lay on my back with my head resting on a couple of pillows, pulled the bedclothes up to my chin, and vowed I would go all the way with the experience, however long it took and wherever it took me.

As it happens, it took quite a long time, somewhere between two and three hours, during which period I reached the consciousness-expanding stage some three or four times, but without going further and being frustratingly returned to my previous reduced mental state. Each time it happened I had to go through the whole wretched procedure again. But then, at last, the interior shaking and shuddering started, and not long afterwards, to my surprise, there erupted a noise that sounded like a rushing wind, which I had not heard before, and as it grew in volume I was suddenly lifted up slightly and then moved down towards the foot of the bed through an intense darkness. I believe I felt exhilaration, but the experience was so sudden, powerful and unexpected, that it didn't really evoke any response in me: I was simply whisked along like a dead leaf, yet without knowing how, and swept, surrounded by that tremendous rushing noise, through the blackness.

This movement lasted for about four or five seconds, I suppose. Then the noise stopped abruptly, and I was no longer in the darkness, but was instead kneeling on all fours on the end of the bed, my body apparently positioned quite the other way around, staring across the room towards the windows on the other side of it. The room was gloomy with the night's darkness but had some city light filtering into it through the windows. I don't remember being startled by where I was, and I felt no different within myself. I could sense, or so it seemed, my arms and legs, although I didn't look to see if they were really there, and seemingly the rest of my body. Yet I lacked any memory of what I'd been trying to do, which perhaps accounts for my calmness and for my inability to take advantage of the situation. The room, I remember, was quite silent.

From my new vantage point I looked somewhat dully at the scene before me, turning my head slowly from left to right, noticing the two windows, the shapes of the pictures on the wall, and various pieces of furniture. I saw nothing unusual until, looking further around to my right, I caught sight of my girlfriend kneeling on the end of the bed beside me. She appeared entirely normal, except that she was illuminated in some strange way, because despite there being very little light in the room, I could see her quite distinctly: her black hair and pale skin, the texture of her nightdress, and the somewhat serious expression of her features. Neither of us spoke, there was simply no time for that, and anyway, I had no desire to say anything. Her face turned with mine, mirroring its movement, so that we looked at one another, and as our eyes met she smiled at me, in a rather slow and gentle manner, without parting her lips, almost as if she was acknowledging some secret that she shared with me.

Then strangely, as her smile widened to its fullest extent and with her eyes looking straight into mine, the whole scene suddenly vanished and I found myself back in bed again, my eyes flicking open at the jolt I felt, to discover that I was lying on my back with the bedclothes pulled up to my chin, in the same position as before. I gasped in wonder and amazement. I had briefly, I realized, left my body and then had been returned to it, just as my girlfriend had done. For she still lay beside me, a barely distinguishable shape in the gloom, breathing quietly, sound asleep.

It seems plain that during this remarkable, if brief, experience the position of my consciousness had shifted from a location just above the pillows supporting my head, to one about six feet away at the opposite end of the bed, and some two feet higher. This had occurred during the movement, which was distinctly sensed, through the darkness, and accompanied by the rushing noise. Yet something else had also been moved, not my physical self, for that remained lying in bed, but my form, which I became aware of when I emerged from the darkness, and which felt so like my physical body that I could not distinguish the difference. But despite this similarity, it was not my physical body, but rather, from what I could sense of its shape, its exact replica, my double.

I do not know how my girlfriend appeared so wonderfully on the end of the bed beside me, except to suggest that either her form had somehow been pulled from her physical body by the outward movement of my own, or that she was aware of what had happened to me at a psychic level and that her form had risen, so to speak, to join me. I certainly saw an exact likeness of her physical self, then sleeping, which was of course her double. But whether it had her consciousness is another matter, because when I told her the next morning about what had happened, she had no recollection at all of having knelt on all fours beside me, although I might have received a different answer had I woken her immediately.

This remarkable experience was not, as some readers might suppose, a dream. Not only did it have an altogether different quality and feel to it, but I had taken particular care not to fall asleep beforehand. And anyway, when we awake from a dream we always know we have been dreaming, even though the dream seems entirely real at the time, whereas I had no such dream-sense afterwards. Its memory has also stayed with me, unlike that of all the dreams, including those I have written down, I have since had.

But if I became my own double, is such duplication the same as astral projection, which is what I was trying to achieve? And can I call it an out-of-body experience, if I was aware of still being in my body? Moreover, if there were two of me and also two versions of my girlfriend, which one is the real me and which the real her, or are both of them real? Certainly the 'me' on all fours felt completely bona fide, while the body on the bed seemed to have no significance at all. And yet if my sleeping girlfriend still retained her consciousness, was the replica who smiled so enigmatically at me just a hologram?

The nature of the double, as these questions suggest, is a fascinating field of enquiry, one that has been sadly neglected by both paranormal researchers and by scientists. I have tried to redress such difficult to understand neglect by presenting a full account of the old beliefs regarding doubles, the details of many of the witnessed accounts of them, both in former times and in the modern world, and also many of their little known characteristics. This should enable you to better understand the answers to these questions, and why what we call reality may not be so real after all.

All in all, I hope the book proves as interesting to read as it was to write.

1 Doubles in Myth and Folklore

For the ghosts of the living walk, I know,
More often than those of the peaceful dead;
Have I not through those alleys seen you go,
A tall, slim girl, with a proud, small head?
From *The Haunting* by Edward Shanks

The strange entity known as the double is, as the name suggests, the exact replica of a living person. Yet it is, none the less, not his (or her) identical twin sibling or someone who happens to bear a striking resemblance to him, but is instead a paranormal likeness that takes its origin from the person, and which has, in this regard, some common ground with a ghost, the likeness of someone who is dead. For this reason doubles have been called 'apparitions of the living'. However, the double of someone who is about to die, or who has recently died, is traditionally called a wraith.

The double is usually dressed in clothes that are replicas of those of the real person, although occasionally they may be of a different style or colour. Its complexion and sometimes its overall colouring, however, are typically somewhat paler, giving it an odd, rather unhealthy appearance. Its posture and way of moving mimic the real person's, and if it speaks its voice is the same. Yet while the double may possess his or her consciousness, and thus be both self-aware and capable of carrying on a conversation, such transference of consciousness does not always occur, which results in the double behaving rather like a zombie. Its separation from the body is also only temporary; thus it cannot remain apart from its physical self and take up an independent existence of its own.

The double may manifest close to the real person, or some distance away – sometimes indeed at a very great distance away. The person's apparent existence in two places at the same time like this is known as *bilocation*, and the double is either projected to that separate site, so that it appears there, as it were, out of thin air, or it may walk there, or it may even, on rare occasions, float there through the air. However, when the double returns to its source it usually just fades into apparent nothingness, and so disappears.

This all sounds, of course, totally impossible, even nonsensical, and many readers will perhaps think that the phenomenon of the double, when reported, is the result of mistaken identity, whereby someone who happens to resemble another is wrongly thought to be him or her. Yet we all know how, when such a sighting occurs, we are always left feeling somewhat uncertain that the person really is whom we suppose him (or her) to be – we suspect, in other words, that our eyes may have deceived us – whereas when a double is seen, the observer is in no doubt about its identity, being quite sure that it's so-and-so, even though so-and-so was somewhere else at the time.

The sightings of doubles also have a long history, which further suggests that they are a real, though mysterious, phenomenon, rather than simply being mistakes in identification. This is why a brief survey of what was known and believed about them, as well as a look at some of their curious appearances, in past times, will not only help to round them out, so to speak, but may provide us with further clues as to their nature and to their purpose.

The earliest references to the human double are found in ancient Egyptian texts, written in hieroglyphics, dating back about 3,500 years before Christ. These reveal that the Egyptians believed our bodies to be formed of three separate yet conjoined parts, which they called the *khat*, the *khu*, and the *ka*. The khat is the familiar physical part of ourselves, which provides a frame or home for the other two, the khu, or soul, and the ka, or spirit, which are quasi-physical. The khu and the ka are, in fact, both doubles, although of different aspects of ourselves.

The khu is somewhat difficult to comprehend, for it has little in common with what we today understand by the term 'soul', being the double, according to the Egyptians, of our will and our thoughts, our ambitions and our desires, which of course have no objective reality, yet none the less exist within us. Hence in a general sense the khu accords with what we now call consciousness, although the Egyptians rather oddly pictured it as residing in the heart, not the brain. The khu left the body at death, when it was said to take the form of a bird.

The ka, or spirit, by contrast, was considered to be the twin or double of the body itself, entering the world with it at birth, and within which, like water in a jug, it resides, although the Egyptians also thought that the ka could separate itself from the body during sleep, notably when we dream, or when we are in a trance or a coma. The ka, they said, projects slightly from the body surface to form its surrounding spiritual envelope, known today as the *aura*, a Greek word meaning 'breeze' or 'breath', which can be seen in favourable lighting conditions. I have observed that my own aura (or ka, if you like) has a thickness of about one tenth of an inch and is completely transparent, although some psychics claim they can see colour in auras, whose hue reflects the health of the person. However, the Egyptians claimed that when seen apart from the body, the ka is identical to it in appearance, with the exception of its paler colouring, and is thought to be that person until it reveals itself, as it may, by its strange demeanour, or by suddenly fading away into nothing.

Moreover, the Egyptians also believed that other animals have both a khu and ka, while plants and non-living things, including manufactured objects, have a ka. Thus everything in nature, according to both them and, indeed, other ancient peoples, possesses a spirit form – although as I have indicated, early man did not regard a spirit as being the wholly nonmaterial entity that we do. And while this likewise sounds unbelievable, it does help explain why ghosts (and doubles, for that matter) are always clothed. For our clothes, if the Egyptians are correct, also have a ka or double, and when we die our body's wraith (from which the ghost, as we shall see, derives) naturally attracts to itself the double of one or other of its favourite outfits, just as it does when it separates itself from the living body. In a similar way, the wraith will take with it and so wear the kas or doubles of its wrist watch, jewellery, spectacles, shoes, wig and so on, which help give it a fully accoutered appearance. The doubles of large manufactured items like cars have also been seen, and are sometimes driven by their owner's double or by his or her wraith!

The existence of the ka or spirit, if not the khu, is further supported by Kirlian photography, which reveals a radiating corona of light, resembling the aura seen by psychics, emanating from the surfaces of both living things and non-living objects, whose thickness and brightness, where the living are concerned, varies depending upon the subject's state of health, both mental and physical. Some scientists think that the corona is a biological plasma, which if true, means that it necessarily has its own energy requirements, which accords with the ancient Egyptian belief that the khu and the ka are nourished by the kas of the foods eaten, in the same way that the body is by their physical substance. Kirlian photography does show a radiant corona emanating from bread, cheese, apples and other foodstuffs, and which of course will, when these are eaten, be ingested; and it has likewise been discovered that the aura of an otherwise healthy subject becomes noticeably less bright when he or she is starved, which suggests that its energy level is lower.

The ancient Greeks were also familiar with doubles, although they originally considered them to be replicas created by the gods for the purpose of deceiving others. Thus we read that when Zeus, the king of the gods, began to suspect that his guest Ixion had lascivious designs on his wife Hera, he made a double of her from a cloud, and watched angrily as Ixion later confirmed his suspicions by embracing the double, thinking she was Hera, and by lying with her. To punish Ixion for so shamelessly abusing his 'wife' and his hospitality, Zeus condemned him to roll a fiery wheel endlessly across the sky, which he is presumably still doing.

Yet although the double that Zeus made, which was named Nephele (meaning 'cloud'), was formed from water vapour, she was none the less substantial enough to feel like the real woman, and sufficiently exact internally to later bear three children to Athamas, the man she eventually married. Hence Nephele did not dissolve away once she had been ravished by Ixion, but retained her feminine form and loveliness for many years afterwards. And as we shall see, such apparent solidity and accompanying internal replication, although not length of existence, is a feature of many doubles.

However, the first god-created double of European literature appears in the *Iliad*, an epic poem composed by Homer in the eighth century BC. The poem deals with the tragic events that happened during a brief period of the Trojan War, fought between about 1194 and 1184 BC, when the Greek hero Achilles, whose honour had been insulted, withdrew from the conflict in a sulk. Not long afterwards, following the breaking of a truce, the Trojan prince Aeneas has his hip smashed with a rock by Diomedes and is removed from the battlefield by the god Apollo, who takes him to Troy to be healed by Leto and Artemis:

Meanwhile Apollo of the Silver Bow created a phantom which looked exactly like Aeneas and was armed as he was. Round this phantom, the Trojans and the brave Achaeans hacked at each other's leather shields (*Iliad*, Book V)

Homer's term for Aeneas's phantom or double is 'eidolon', which also means an 'image' or a 'representation'. In the

23

latter sense it was later used to describe man-made statues or images of the gods. It is from this use of eidolon, by contraction, that our English word 'idol' derives. Moreover, while in early times the diphthong 'ei' of eidolon was pronounced as 'ay' and the 'd' like the short 'd' of the word 'dog', later the diphthong came to be sounded as 'ee' and the 'd' as 'th', so that the word as a whole was pronounced 'eetholon', from which our English word 'heathen' derives, meaning an image or eidolon worshipper.

The cause of the Trojan War was the abduction by Paris (a son of King Priam of Troy) of Helen, the wife of Menelaus, king of Sparta, to Troy, which is why she is familiarly known as Helen of Troy. Yet some Greeks asserted, perhaps not entirely without reason, that Helen never went to Troy, but was instead removed at Zeus's command to Egypt, where she remained throughout the ten-year conflict. Her place was taken, they claimed, by a double, made from clouds by Hera. The ersatz Helen was unsuspectingly carried off to Troy by Paris, on whom he fathered, like Athamas with Nephele, several children, which likewise suggests that as a replica she was complete in every way.

This early Greek belief that doubles are made from clouds may have arisen because many doubles, as I have already pointed out, are projected to the spot where they are seen, so that they appear to materialize, as if by magic, from out of thin air, like clouds.

Perhaps the most famous ancient account of someone undergoing repeated double separations is described by the Roman writer Pliny the Elder (AD 23–79) in his *Natural History*, although when exactly the man in question lived is uncertain.

Pliny records that in the Greek colonial city of Clazomenae, sited on the coast of Asia Minor (now western Turkey) and founded in 656 BC, an inhabitant named Hermotinus frequently fell into a swoon or trance, whereupon his double left his body and travelled about the world, meeting all sorts of people and bringing back 'numerous accounts of various things, which could not have been obtained by any one but a person who was present'. Unfortunately, however, during one of Hermotinus's out-of-body excursions someone (who was either his fed-up wife or a bitter enemy) set fire to, and killed, his abandoned physical shell, which robbed his double of its natural home and obliged it to travel on to wherever the spirits of the dead go. The murdered Hermotinus, who had been highly regarded by his fellow citizens, was awarded divine honours in one of Clazomenae's temples, from which women were banned by law. Thus he had, one might say, a form of recompense.

Herodotus (*c.* 480–425 BC), the most illustrious and readable of ancient Greek historians, describes the appearance of a double in his *The Histories*, which, if true, shows that the doubles of men are just as capable of having sex (with full-bodied women) and procreating children, as women's doubles are of becoming pregnant and giving birth! The incident in question happened shortly before the invasion of Greece by Darius, the Persian king, in 504 BC.

Apparently one Demaratus, who believed himself to be the son and heir of Ariston, the king of Sparta, was told by his brother during an argument, that their mother, when she married Ariston, was already pregnant with him, and that his real father was either her previous husband or, worse still, one of his grooms. This accusation was seemingly confirmed by the Delphic oracle, to which Demaratus applied in order to learn the truth about his paternity, whose priestess Perialla told him that Ariston was certainly not his real father, although it was later proved she had been bribed to say that.

On his return to Sparta, the distressed Demaratus implored his mother to tell him under oath what the truth was, complaining that he had even heard that Ariston was impotent and thus incapable of fathering him. Demaratus's mother, seeing her son's anguish, answered him by saying that the physical Ariston wasn't his father, yet he had been conceived by his double, which meant that Ariston, in this regard, was his progenitor.

'On the third night after Ariston brought me to his house,' she explained, 'I was visited in my room by a phantom exactly resembling him. The phantom came to my bed, and afterwards took the wreath it was wearing and put it about my brows. Then it vanished, and when Ariston came in later, he asked who had given me the wreath. I said that he had given it me himself, but he denied it: then I solemnly swore that it was so, and reproached him for his denial, since so short a time before he had had me in his arms and given me the wreath.'

This story is so wonderfully fantastic that it almost has to be true, for it brilliantly answers every doubt that Demaratus had about his paternity, but if it is not, and I am sure that many readers will at this stage find it hard to believe, it is surely the most ingenious excuse that a cheating woman, who became pregnant, ever thought up.

And interestingly, Herodotus's story finds an echo in the account given by Geoffrey of Monmouth of how Merlin's mother, who was a nun, conceived her son. When asked by Vortigern, the British king, how this happened, she replied, without blushing, that she had not had intercourse with an ordinary male, which would have been a sin, but rather with 'the form of a most handsome young man' who used to visit her in her cell. 'He would often hold me tightly in his arms and kiss me,' she added. 'Many times, too, when I was sitting alone, he would talk with me, without becoming visible; and when he came to see me in this way he would often make love with me, as a man would do, and in that way he made me pregnant.'

In about AD 53, the apostle Paul, accompanied by Silas, revisited a number of cities in Asia Minor, where he had previously converted many to Christianity and had founded churches, to offer advice and to give comfort to the new recruits. However, when Paul and Silas had worked their way through the provinces of Phrygia and Galatia to Troas, in the north-west of what is now Turkey, they were uncertain of where best to proceed from there. It was during this period of indecision that Paul was apparently visited by someone's double:

> And a vision appeared to Paul in the night; There stood a man of Macedonia, and prayed him, saying, Come over into Macedonia, and help us.
> And after he had seen the vision, immediately we endeavoured to go into Macedonia, assuredly gathering that the Lord had called us for to preach the gospel unto them. (*The Acts*, Chapter XVI, vv. 9, 10)

As we shall discover later, one of the reasons why the double leaves the body of a person, in order to visit another or others at a distant place, is because he is worried either for himself or for the person visited. And early Christians had much cause for anxiety, for they were not only unpopular with, and persecuted by, their pagan fellow citizens, but they were operating in a vacuum, so to speak, having no one to turn to for guidance, let alone encouragement. Hence it is perhaps not surprising that Paul should be visited in this way, by the double of a distraught Macedonian Christian, who was either already known to him or who was able to identify himself in his duplicate form. And the double's startling appearance was successful, for Paul and Silas left immediately for Macedonia, where they brought new hope to their beleaguered co-religionists.

The reason why Paul was seemingly unsurprised by, and accepting of, the man of Macedonia's double, was because he had undergone something similar himself only seven years previously, which he describes (in the third person singular) in his *Second Letter to the Corinthians*, and which, bearing in mind my own initial uncertainty about whether I was out of my body or not, has all the hallmarks of a double projection, although one that took Paul's replica far beyond the confines of his bedroom.

And I knew such a man, (whether in the body, or out of the body, I cannot tell: God knoweth;)

How that he was caught up into paradise, and heard unspeakable words, which it is not lawful for a man to utter.

Of such an one will I glory: yet of myself I will not glory, but in mine infirmities. (II *Corinthians*, Chapter XII, vv. 3–5)

Furthermore, the apocryphal *Acts of John* refers to the double of Jesus, which was apparently seen on several occasions by the apostle. The term 'apocryphal', according to Montague Rhodes James, the translator of the *Acts of John*, does not mean the writings are spurious. Indeed, they were originally considered to be too sacred and secret for none but the eyes of initiates. The *Acts of John* date from the middle of the second century AD, and they are attributed to Leucius, one of John's disciples. This is what they record John as saying happened when he stayed with Jesus and the other disciples one night at a house in Gennesaret:

I alone having wrapped myself in my mantle, watched what he should do: and first I heard him say: John, go thou to sleep. And I thereon feigning to sleep saw another like unto him, whom also I heard say unto my Lord: Jesus, they whom thou hast chosen believe not yet on thee. And my Lord said unto him: Thou sayest well: for they are men. (*Acts of John*, v. 92)

What makes this incident particularly interesting and unusual is that Jesus's double, the 'another like unto him', actually speaks to Jesus, so that the Lord both sees and converses with himself. And significantly, John later discloses that Jesus did not always feel the same when touched, a difference that presumably came about because he sometimes encountered Jesus's double, rather than the real man. Leucius reports

John as saying: 'Sometimes when I would lay hold of him, I met with a material and solid body, and at other times, again, when I felt him, the substance was immaterial and as if it existed not at all.' (*Acts of John*, v. 93)

And while the double, by its very name and nature, is generally an exact replica of the real person, this is not always the case, as I shall discuss at length in a later chapter. The ability of the double to change its form would seemingly explain why Jesus was seen by John and others as having a different appearance on several occasions. Indeed, it sometimes happened, as mentioned below, that two people would see him at the same time in a different guise:

> When we departed from that place, being minded to follow him, again he was seen of me as having a head rather bald, but the beard thick and flowing, but of James as a youth whose beard was newly come. We were therefore perplexed, both of us, as to what that which we had seen should mean .. And oft-times he would appear to me as a small man and uncomely, and then again as one reaching to heaven. (*Acts of John*, v. 89)

And on another occasion, Jesus is seen as having the characteristic pallor of a double, which naturally suggests that he was then in this form, particularly as he undergoes another transformation moments later:

> I, therefore, because he loved me, drew nigh unto him softly, as though he could not see *me*, and stood looking upon his hinder parts: and I saw that he was not in any wise clad with garments, but was seen of us naked, and not in any wise as a man, and that his feet were whiter than any snow, so that the earth was lighted up by his feet, and that his head touched unto heaven: so that I was afraid and cried out, and he, turning about, appeared as a man of small stature, and caught hold of

my beard and pulled it and said: John, be not faithless but believing, and not curious. (*Acts of John*, v. 90)

As we have seen, the Greeks of former times called the double an eidolon, as indeed they still do today, while the Romans referred to it, perhaps not surprisingly, as a *simulacrum*. We are most familiar nowadays with its German name of *doppelgänger* or 'double-goer' because during the nineteenth century, when some celebrated cases of double appearances in Germany received a lot of publicity, it became an adopted term for the phenomenon. The French call the double *un fantôme*, while in Sweden it is known as a *fylgja*, meaning 'the follower' or 'the second', and in Norway as a *vardogr*, or 'following spirit'.

During the eighteenth century and the first half of the nineteenth, the double was generally referred to as a 'fetch' throughout Ireland and much of England, although the term was used somewhat interchangeably with wraith, and it evidently entered our vocabulary around the year 1700, despite there being, as there still are, various local words for the phenomenon. In Cumberland, for example, the double was called a 'swarth' which means 'dark' and which refers to its often malignant significance. Further north, in Northumberland, the double was known as a 'waff' and in Scotland as a 'fye'.

It was a common belief that the double, when seen in the evening or during the hours of darkness, foretold the coming death of the person whose likeness it was, whereas if the sighting occurred earlier in the day, a happier outcome was signified. The appearance of someone's double in the morning, for example, betokened good health and a long life for that person. However, it was, and still is, regarded as a malevolent omen for anyone to see his own likeness, as this invariably presaged his death.

The following verses, quoted by William Hone in *The Every-Day Book*, describe how a widowed man was forewarned of the death of his only daughter, while out for a walk alone, by the sight of the girl's double:

One evening I left her asleep in her smiles,
And walked through the mountains, lonely;
I was far from my darling, ah! many long miles,
And I thought of her, and her only;

She darkened my path like a troubled dream,
In that solitude far and drear;
I spoke to my child! but she did not seem
To hearken with human ear

She only looked with a dead, dead eye,
And a wan, wan cheek of sorrow –
I knew her 'fetch'! she was called to die,
And she died upon the morrow.

In some areas of the world, however, such as the Pacific Islands, the double of a loved one is said to augur death only when the person who sees it fails to recognize the likeness for what it is, which is easily done, and either kisses it or makes some other form of intimate contact with it. Such a fatal mistake is revealed by the double fading away before the horror-struck victim's eyes, who knows by his act that he has but three days left to live.

According to English tradition, there are two dates in the Christian calendar when the doubles of those who are destined to die can invariably be seen. This symbolic display of coming calamity occurs on 24 April, or St Mark's Eve, and on 23 June, or St John's Eve, otherwise known as Midsummer Eve.

On both occasions the ghoulishly curious, having spent the day fasting, must seat themselves within the porch of their local church at 11 p.m., where they will see, at or around midnight, the doubles or 'death-fetches' of all those parishioners destined to die in the following year walk up to the church door, in the same order as their respective demises, and enter the church. However, this procession of doubles can only be witnessed on St Mark's Eve by those who have

31

watched out for them on the same date in the two previous years. Hence it is third time lucky for them, although unlucky for those who are seen. But owing to the large populations of many city parishes, it is probable nowadays that only the doubles of those members of the church congregation who are about to die turn up.

Yet be warned that a church-watcher must be prepared for some rather grim sights, as the double of anyone who is going to die a violent death will show signs of this in its appearance and manner. Thus the double of someone destined to be drowned, for example, will enter the church porch struggling and thrashing, as if with the water that will soon close over his head; the double of someone who will hang himself will enter with mouth agape and a protruding tongue, and with a purple-coloured face; the double of a coming victim of a heroin overdose will have a sleeve rolled up to reveal the punctured veins in its arm and its eyes will be wild and staring; and the double of a car driver fated to be killed in an accident will arrive with shattered limbs and a body covered in blood, and with the sad look of someone who knew he shouldn't have been speeding but who was too stupid to slow down. And so on.

The brother of one female church-watcher told William Hone how his sister had had the misfortune to see her own likeness arrive at the church door:

I am sure that my own sister Hetty, who died just before Christmas, stood in the church-porch last Midsummer eve, to see all who were about to die that year in our parish; and she saw her own apparition.

But none the less, St Mark's Eve can also be used for happier ends, as on this night unmarried women may discover if they are to marry in the coming year, and if so, who their husband will be. And no previous visits to the church porch on that date are required!

The inquisitive maiden, in the early evening of 24 April,

must take to the church porch either a large flower (a tulip, St Mark's flower, is ideal) or a small branch cut from a tree (preferably one Venus-ruled, like alder, cherry, elder, sweet chestnut, or sycamore), which she will leave there as a marker. Then, shortly before midnight, she must return to the porch alone, take up her flower or branch, and, sitting in the darkness, quietly watch for any supernatural display.

If she is to marry in the next twelvemonth, she will, when midnight has struck, soon see a wedding procession pass by, which will be led by her own double, wearing a bridal gown, arm-in-arm with that of the man she is to marry. The number of youths and girls making up the spectral procession behind her double will together reveal the number of months that shall pass before the happy event. Yet the sight of this visitation must prompt no screams, faints, or seizures of terror on the part of the watching virgin, as these will lead to a dissolution of the phantoms, and possibly a change in what is to be. And clearly, if no doubles are seen by her at all, then she must expect matrimonial disappointment in the year ahead.

Should an unmarried woman wish to see the phantom likeness of her husband-to-be, without sitting in a church porch at midnight, which is not for the faint-hearted, then she may do this at home in the company of two or more of her friends, by turning with them her and their shifts or petticoats, although at the same late hour. This procedure is carried out on 6 May, once dedicated to St Mark but now to St John the Evangelist. In 1791, at Hingham in Norfolk, two cheeky young men took advantage of some tremulous maidens who hoped to see the doubles of their future spouses, by stealing their petticoats, as described below:

On Friday the 6th inst. being Old St Mark's day, four young damsels at Hingham, anxious to know the men who were to lead them to the Hymeneal altar, agreed to *watch their shifts*, as it is called, at night, having an idea, that if they hung them turned inside out, in a room, wherein themselves were to sit with the doors and win-

33

dows open, and not to speak to each other, the men who are to be their husbands would come at midnight and *turn* them – having hung them as directed, the important hour of midnight arrived – when lo! two young men, disguised, who had previously heard of their intent, entered the room, and having *turned* the shifts *to their own account*, decamped with them, leaving the poor *shiftless* damsels to lament their loss. (*The Norfolk Chronicle*, Saturday, 14 May 1791)

Alternatively, if you wish to see the double of your husband-to-be at home alone, you need only fast throughout 23 June, or Midsummer Eve, and then, at midnight, place a clean cloth on your dining room table, and lay on it a loaf of fresh bread, a large piece of cheese, an uncapped bottle of brown ale, and a glass. You must next open the front door, then return to the table, likewise leaving your dining room door open behind you, and sit down as if you were about to refresh youself, but without touching anything. If you wait quietly, it won't be long (always assuming that you will one day marry) before the wished-for double appears, who will enter the room, nod respectfully towards you, to acknowledge your presence, fill the glass with beer, and without touching either the food or the beverage, nod in your direction again, then disappear. You may then rise and shut the doors, and afterwards eat and drink your fill, which might help stop you from screaming the house down.

This brief look at the double from an historical perspective reveals it to be an entity of some apparent contradiction. It apparently normally exists within our physical body, yet it can occasionally step out from the body and wander about alone, when it may act and speak like the real person or alternatively behave like a zombie. It possesses many of the properties of physical matter, which allow it to be seen and to manipulate physical objects, and which may even include the ability to enjoy procreative couplings with ordinary people, yet it can suddenly appear like a ghost from out of thin air, and at a distant place, from whence it eventually vanishes, to return to its owner, just as mysteriously. Again, the sighting of a double may lack any predictive significance whatsoever, or it may be the forerunner of some happy event, or alternatively it may portend the death of the person who sees it or the one whose likeness it is. And occasionally, someone may see his own double, yet without being aware that it has departed from his body.

2 Doubles of the Dying

Now do I know
How newly-dead men go
As ragged ghosts among familiar ways,
Seeking to live again remembered days.
         From *No More That Road* by John Freeman

In the last chapter I mentioned that when someone's double is seen at night it is said to presage the death of the person whose likeness it is, which is why it was formerly called a death-fetch. This belief is not a superstition; rather, it derives from the repeated sightings, over a period of many millennia, of people's doubles either shortly before, or sometimes shortly after, their demise. This of course points to the reality of the double, although some have argued, as we shall see, that it only reveals the impression of the double in the witnesses' minds, and not its external objectivity.

The reason why the appearance of a double at night became regarded as an omen of death is because most deaths take place at night. And while the doubles that by tradition walk up to a church porch at midnight portend the deaths, in the year ahead, of those whose likeness they have, it is far commoner for a double to be unexpectedly seen either by a family member or by a close friend in their own home or at their work place, shortly before the person's death. This suggests that as death approaches the double undergoes a loosening of its connections within the physical body, perhaps somewhat in the manner that I experienced when I tried to 'astrally project', which allows it to vacate the body before the latter's heart has stopped beating and to be projected to the place where it is seen. In this way it can serve as a forerunner. However, it is often impossible to be sure whether the sighting took place before or after the heart ceased to beat. This is particularly true when the double is seen at a distant place.

Yet the externalized double does not always pay visits to friends or loved ones, or to church porches for that matter, but may instead wander somewhat aimlessly around the place where the physical body is lying.

One of the most remarkable examples of a deathbed duplication happened to Queen Elizabeth I, who not only saw her own double shortly before she expired, but who was also seen afterwards in double form by one of her ladies-in-waiting. The great queen had gone into a sudden decline in March 1603, at Richmond in Surrey, when she was in her seventieth year, yet she was so afraid to lie down, for fear that she would never get up again, that despite feeling very unwell, she stayed awake and out of bed for a whole week, before finally succumbing to her weakness and weariness, and becoming bed-ridden, on the first day of spring. She died three days later on Thursday, 24 March, having ruled her island kingdom for a little over 44 years.

During those final three days, Elizabeth was constantly watched over by her tremulous ladies-in-waiting, who took turns at the task, and who, owing to the fact that their royal mistress either slept or maintained an incommunicative silence when awake, found the job alternately boring and nerve-racking. The strain proved too much for Lady Guildford, who, in order to break the tedium and to obtain a breath of fresher air, audaciously stepped out of Elizabeth's chamber for a few minutes, when her charge had sunk into a deep sleep. What she saw outside shocked her into quickly returning.

Lady Guildford . . . leaving her in an almost breathless sleep in her privy-chamber [writes Agnes Strickland], went to take a little air, and met her Majesty, as she

37

thought, three or four chambers off. Alarmed at the thought of being discovered in the act of leaving the royal patient alone, she hurried forward, in some trepidation, in order to excuse herself, when the apparition vanished away. Lady Guildford returned, terrified, to the chamber, but there lay Queen Elizabeth still in the same lethargic motionless slumber, in which she had left her.

Figure 1   Queen Elizabeth's double was not amused!

Lady Guildford's experience is a fairly typical example of a double sighting. She apparently sees her dying mistress standing in a place apart from where she actually is, yet looking exactly the same, so that there is no way for her to tell that the double is not the real person. Startled and guilt-stricken, the lady-in-waiting goes towards the likeness, which vanishes before she reaches it, thereby revealing to her that it is not the real woman. The double neither says, nor does, anything to indicate why it is there, although we may perhaps surmise that the sleeping queen, who was never left unattended unless she desired solitude, was able to detect at a subconscious level Lady Guildford's absence from her chamber, and that her double spontaneously projected itself to the spot where her errant lady-in-waiting was, to remind her that such liberties were not permitted.

Something equally strange and oddly significant happened

three days after Elizabeth had died. Her body, having been treated with preservatives and wrapped in a shroud, was taken on 26 March from Richmond to Whitehall, and the next day it was nailed up in a wooden coffin decorated with lead leaves, which was afterwards covered in velvet. Then later that night (27 March), while the coffin was attended by several women, Elizabeth's corpse burst with a loud bang and with such force that it cracked open the coffin, scattering the women in terror. The explosion was doubtless caused by a build-up of gases within the decomposing monarch's body, so inflating it to bursting point like an over-expanded balloon, although the weather was hardly warm enough for such rapid decomposition.

I mention this curious fact because it was an amazing omen, hitherto unreported, of the destruction that lay ahead for the monarchy. For in 1625, on the same date that Elizabeth's corpse blew up, namely 27 March, King Charles I ascended the throne. This monarch's absolutism eventually led to the social explosion of the English civil war, which ended with his defeat and his subsequent trial and execution. At daybreak prior to Charles's beheading (which took place on 30 January 1649, also at Whitehall, where Elizabeth's body had exploded) the bishop in attendance read the twenty-seventh chapter of St Matthew's gospel, the lesson for that day, whose content, the crucifixion of Jesus Christ, both deeply moved and comforted the king. And scarcely less astonishing is the fact that I discovered these strange coincidences on 27 March!

Queen Elizabeth I, who was unmarried and incapable of having sexual intercourse, owing to her unusually thick hymen, which perhaps not surprisingly, there being no effective anaesthetics available, she declined to have surgically removed, left no heir, and was succeeded by her cousin twice removed, the estimable James VI of Scotland, who became James I of England, France and Ireland. The new monarch left Edinburgh on 11 April, and arrived in the capital on 7 May. Shortly afterwards, on 11 May 1603, wishing to ingratiate himself with the English people and nobility, King James created 133 new knights, one of whom was Robert Cotton, who resided at Connington, in Huntingdonshire.

During the summer of that year the plague broke out in London, prompting many citizens to flee the city for the relative safety of the country. Two such absentees were William Camden (1551–1623), the historian and antiquary, and Ben Jonson (1572–1639), then England's most famous poet and playwright, who lodged with the newly-knighted Sir Robert Cotton at Connington, although Jonson had somewhat churlishly left behind his wife and children at home in Westminster.

Early on the morning of 11 September, in his bedroom at Connington, Ben Jonson was shocked to see the figure of his eldest son, a boy of only seven years of age, standing close by his bed, with what appeared to be 'the mark of a bloodie cross on his forehead, as if it had been cutted with a sword'. The dreadful figure persisted for some minutes before disappearing. Later, at sunrise, the shaken playwright, alarmed that the vision portended the death of his favourite child, went to Camden's bedroom and told him what he had seen, yet was persuaded by the older man that it was nothing but a fantasy created by his anxiety, and that he should not be discomforted by it. But Camden was wrong, for not long afterwards Jonson received a letter from his wife bearing the tragic news that the boy had died of the plague.

Hence Ben Jonson had been visited by the wraith of his son, which manifested in his bedroom at or about the time of the boy's death, although it differed from the real child in having the mark of a bloody cross on its forehead. The latter sign served to symbolize the boy's death or approaching death from the plague, for a red cross was painted on the doors of houses where such deaths had occurred, to warn others that the building was infected. Its presence may therefore be explained by supposing that the dying boy knew his house would soon be decorated with such a cross, and that this knowledge somehow spontaneously created the mark on his double's forehead.

In memory of the child, and no doubt to lessen the feelings of guilt that persisted within him for years afterwards, Jonson wrote the following epigram on his death:

> *Farewell, thou child of my right hand, and joy;*
> *My sin was too much hope of thee, loved boy.*
> *Seven years thou wert lent to me, and I thee pay,*
> *Exacted by thy fate, on the just day.*
> *O, could I lose all father now! For why*
> *Will man lament the state he should envy?*
> *To have so soon 'scaped world's and flesh's rage,*
> *And, if no other misery, yet age?*
> *Rest in soft peace, and, asked, say here doth lie*
> *Ben Jonson, his best piece of poetry.*
> *For whose sake, henceforth, all vows be such*
> *As what he loved may never like too much.*

Not long afterwards, in 1611, the poet John Donne had a similar experience at Paris, where he went as companion to the new Ambassador Sir Robert Drury. And remarkably, Donne had been lodging with Sir Robert at his house in the eponymous Drury Lane, London (although he had his wife Anne with him), which meant that when his host requested his attendance upon him at Paris, the poet, conscious of the

Figure 2   A shocked John Donne saw the doubles of his wife and child

many favours that he had received from Sir Robert, felt obliged to accompany him, despite his unwillingness to leave his
wife behind, who was heavy with child and who did not want
him to be away from her. Sir Robert, however, being anxious
to have his company, gave Donne little choice in the matter.

Two days after their safe arrival in Paris (and two weeks
after their departure from London), John Donne was left
briefly alone in the room where he and the Ambassador had
dined with their host. But when Sir Robert Drury returned to
the dining room he found that Donne, much to his astonishment, was in a dreadful state, white-faced and shaking, and
looking exactly as if he'd seen a ghost. The knight took his
arm and anxiously demanded what on earth had happened to
upset him so. John Donne did not reply immediately, but
then, gathering himself with an apparent effort of will, he
answered: 'I have seen a dreadful vision since I saw you: I
have seen my dear wife pass twice by me through this room,
with her hair hanging about her shoulders, and a dead child
in her arms; this I have seen since I saw you.'

Taken aback, Sir Robert gasped that his friend must have
fallen asleep in his absence and had had an awful dream.
Donne grimaced and shook his head, then murmured: 'I cannot be surer that I now live, than that I have not slept since I
saw you, and am sure that at her second appearing, she stopt
and lookt at me in the face and vanished.'

Sir Robert insisted that Donne get some rest, supposing
that the strain of their journey, allied with the poet's concern
for his pregnant wife, had somehow combined together to
create an illusion in his mind, which had been seen as the two
external figures. Yet when Donne the next day reaffirmed the
vision in even more detail and expressed a fear that it signified the death of his child, Sir Robert sent a servant back to
London, with orders that he should enquire about the health
of Anne Donne, and that of her infant, if yet born. The man
returned twelve days later, and reported that Donne's wife,
after having endured a very difficult labour, had given birth
to a still-born child, and that she herself was still confined to

bed, suffering from grief, depression, and weakness. Even more remarkably, the time of the birth coincided with the sighting of the doubles of his wife and a child by John Donne.

These three cases, despite their occurrence in the early years of the seventeenth century, retain their interest because they involved famous but otherwise rational persons, the first of whom, namely Queen Elizabeth I, produced a double, while Ben Jonson and John Donne saw doubles of members of their own families, about whom they were experiencing some anxiety. However, before leaving that distant century, there is another fascinating case that happened during it which is worth considering in some detail, not least because it involved ordinary citizens.

In May 1691, a woman named Mary Goffe, of Rochester in Kent, the mother of two young children and the victim of a long and intractable illness, was taken by her husband John to stay with her parents, who lived nine miles away at West Malling, in the hope that the change of scene and the country air might prove beneficial to her. Their children, in the meantime, remained at home with a nurse, the reliable Widow Alexander. Yet despite his best intentions, John Goffe's hope was not matched by any improvement in his wife's condition; in fact it worsened, and Mary died on 4 June.

The night before she died Mary Goffe became very anxious to see her children again, and begged her husband to hire a horse and take her home upon it. John said that that was impossible, as she was too ill to ride or to make such a long journey. A church minister was then brought in to comfort Mary, whom she told that while she was willing to die, she was very upset at being separated from her children. Then later, sometime between one and two o'clock in the morning, according to the woman who sat with her, the agitated Mary fell into a trance-like sleep, one that seemed akin to death, and lay with both her mouth and her eyes open, staring fixedly, yet apparently unseeingly, at the ceiling beams above her. No breath could be detected coming from her mouth or nose.

In the morning, however, Mary Goffe regained consciousness and told her mother, to the latter's surprise, that she had been at her home with her children. Her mother corrected her, saying that she had been in bed all night long. Mary smiled and replied that while that was true, she had nonetheless been with her children when she was asleep. Neither her mother nor her husband knew what to make of this strange announcement, although a day or two afterwards, when John Goffe returned home, the Widow Alexander told him that Mary was not mistaken, however impossible it seemed. Thomas Tilson (the church minister, who recorded the incident) writes:

That a little before two-a-clock that morning, she saw the likeness of the said Mary Goffe come out of the next chamber (where the elder child lay in a bed by itself, the door being left open), and stood by her bed-side for about a quarter of an hour: the younger child was there lying by her: her eyes moved, and her mouth went, but she said nothing. The nurse moreover says, that she was perfectly awake, it was daylight, being one of the longest days in the year. She sate up in her bed, and looked steadfastly upon the apparition; in that time she heard the bridge-clock strike two, and a while after she said, 'In the name of the Father, Son, and Holy Ghost, what art thou?' Thereupon the appearance removed, and went away; she slipp'd on her cloaths and followed, but what became on't she cannot tell.

This case likewise indicates that it is the heartfelt desire of the dying person to be with a particular loved one or loved ones, in this instance the children of the woman concerned, that seemingly prompts the projection of his or her double to the place where they are. The function of the double in this regard is to convey the essence of the dying person to where he or she could not physically be. Indeed, Mary Goffe's double was not only visible to her children and to their nurse, but it also contained her consciousness, which enabled her to participate fully in the experience. Hence it served in a most beautiful way as a substitute for the real person, thereby bringing great comfort to the dying woman.

John Goffe had married Mary (*née* Carpenter) on 12 February 1684 at Aylesford, Kent, and while their marriage was evidently a happy one and he was distraught at her passing, it wasn't long before the bereft widower found someone else. She was also a Kent girl, by name Susanna Everest, and John married her at the village of Snodland on 19 November 1691.

While Queen Elizabeth's double was encountered only a few yards from the dying monarch, the other doubles mentioned above appeared many miles distant from the people whose likeness they were. Mary Goffe's double, for example, was seen at Rochester, nine miles from West Malling, where the real Mary lay close to death; the double of Ben Jonson's son revealed itself to his father, who was staying at Connington, about 60 miles away from London; and the doubles of Anne Donne and her dead child showed themselves to John Donne when he was in Paris, some 225 miles away from London. In each case the appearance of the double was equally life-like, which suggests that distance does not diminish it or impede whatever force projects it to the place where it is seen.

Yet if 225 miles, or even 60 miles, seem excessive and improbable distances to which a double can be projected, there are many cases on record of a double appearing much further away, whereby the people concerned were separated by oceans or by continental land-masses. One of the most remarkable of such distant appearances of a wraith was witnessed by an eighteenth-century English sea-captain at Table Bay in the Cape of Good Hope (then known as Cape Bona Esperance), South Africa, situated some 6,200 miles away from the person whose likeness it was, namely his wife.

Captain Nathaniel Hancock was commander of the East India Company's vessel *Norfolk*, which anchored in Table

Bay on New Year's Day 1747, while en route from England to Madras in India, and where she remained until 4 April. One day Captain Hancock dined ashore in the Dutch colony with some friends, and during the meal, to everyone else's surprise, he suddenly rose from the table and went to the window, through which he stared for several minutes. When he returned, somewhat ashen-faced, to his seat, his fellow diners asked what had caused him to rise so hastily, and he replied by enquiring if any of the company had seen a lady looking in through the window. When all replied that they had not, Captain Hancock sighed, then said: 'I can assure you there was one, and it was my wife.'

This strange remark brought a burst of laughter from his companions, who thought he was joking with them. Yet the captain, with a solemn shake of his head, interrupted their mirth by adding: 'It makes so strong impression on my mind that I will immediately enter the circumstance in my memorandum book, and you will all oblige me, if you would do the same.'

When the *Norfolk* eventually returned to England in August 1748, a close friend of Nathaniel Hancock came on board and sought him out, and the captain, seeing his tense expression, immediately said that he knew why he had come, for he brought news of Mrs Hancock's death. And Captain Hancock went on to mention when, and at what time, the sad event had occurred. His friend stared at him in astonishment, and mumblingly asked how he could possibly know of such a distant happening so exactly, for all he said was correct. The captain sadly took up his memorandum book, and replied that while at dinner on that day, in the faraway Cape of Good Hope, he had seen his wife's wraith gaze in at him through the window, which told him, without any doubt, of her departure from the world.

Nathaniel Hancock was born at Holsworthy in Devon on 27 February 1707, and both his county of birth and date of birth (he was a Piscean) seemingly marked him out for a life at sea. He worked his way up through the ranks and served aboard a variety of East India Company vessels. He was fourth mate of the *Derby* from 1734–35, for example, and second mate of the *Heathcote* from 1739–40. In the lacuna between those two voyages he married Elizabeth Hardyman, who became his second wife, on 17 November 1736, and who died when the *Norfolk* was in Table Bay. His first wife, Bettey Bult (whom he married at age nineteen in 1726), also died young. Yet Nathaniel not only took a third wife, but lived to be eighty years old, dying at Hertford on 5 July 1787.

The *Norfolk*'s period of service with the East India Company lasted from 1745–56, during which time she made four voyages to and from either India or China. She had a weight of only 499 tons, yet she carried a crew of 100. Strangely, and perhaps significantly, the fourth mate on the voyage that took the ship to Table Bay was named David Jones. And equally oddly, on the day after the *Norfolk* arrived there, another Company vessel, the *Porto Bello*, turned up, whose commander was actually a Captain Hook, and he brought news that Madras had been taken by the French. This apparently necessitated a change of the *Norfolk*'s destination from Madras to Benkulen in Sumatra and then to Whampoa, the European port of Canton, in China.

Another and more recent example of such long-distance projection also happened, but off-shore, in faraway South Africa, although the wraith that appeared there belonged to a man who had died two weeks earlier. It manifested in the cabin occupied by the man's brother, Harold Owen, an officer aboard HMS *Astraea*, which was then sailing north from Table Bay, a few days after the First World War ended on 11 November 1918.

The dead sibling was the poet Wilfred Owen, who had had the misfortune to be killed by machine-gun fire in France on 4 November of that year. Harold Owen had no idea that anything untoward had happened to him, although he did recall feeling increasingly anxious about his brother from 11 November onwards, which was the day, interestingly enough, when his parents were informed of Wilfred's death. Harold's anxiety was worsened by a bout of malaria, which turned it into a deep depression, and which prompted the young man to spend time alone in his cabin. Then one evening, on returning to his cabin to write some letters, he was startled to find that his brother Wilfred was apparently waiting in there for him.

I drew aside the door curtain and stepped inside and to my amazement I saw Wilfred sitting in my chair. I felt shock run through me with appalling force and with it I could feel the blood draining away from my face ... I did not sit down but looking at him I spoke quietly: 'Wilfred, how did you get here?' He did not rise and I saw that he was involuntarily immobile, but his eyes which had never left mine were alive with the familiar look of trying to make me understand; when I spoke his whole face broke into his sweetest and most endearing dark smile ... I spoke again: 'Wilfred dear, how can you be here? It's just not possible ...' But still he did not speak but only smiled his most gentle smile ... He was in uniform and I remember thinking how out of place the khaki looked amongst the cabin furnishings. With this thought I must have turned my eyes away from him; when I looked back my cabin chair was empty.

Wilfred Owen's wraith was indistinguishable from the real person, and moreover it was dressed in the army uniform that his brother would have expected to see him in. Indeed, it was only Harold Owen's inner realization that Wilfred could not possibly really be there that told him, contrary to the evidence of his senses, that something was not quite right. The wraith was evidently aware of where it was, and it responded to Harold's questions by smiling, although like many wraiths it did not, and evidently could not, speak. Its appearance, however, was seemingly intended to remove Harold's uncertainty about Wilfred's fate and to end the depression this was causing. And indeed after seeing the wraith Harold comments that he 'knew with absolute certainty that Wilfred was dead'.

What is equally astonishing is that in his best-known poem, entitled *Strange Meeting*, in which Wilfred Owen pictures himself meeting the wraith of a German soldier he had killed the day before, and which eerily smiles at him. He writes:

> *It seemed that out of battle I escaped*
> *Down some profound dull tunnel, long since scooped*
> *Through granites which titanic wars had groined.*
> *Yet also there encumbered sleepers groaned,*
> *Too fast in thought or death to be bestirred.*
> *Then, as I probed them, one sprang up, and stared*
> *With piteous recognition in fixed eyes,*
> *Lifting distressful hands as if to bless.*
> *And by his smile I knew that sullen hall,*
> *By his dead smile I knew we stood in Hell.*

The stare and the smile of the imagined wraith are the exact opposite of those given by Wilfred Owen's real one, which leads me to suspect that another reason for his appearance to his brother was to show him (and us) that his former fear about the next world, as expressed in *Strange Meeting*, is wrong and that no such dark, hopeless place as Hell exists.

But while we can appreciate how the wraith of the dying Elizabeth Hancock may have been projected to such an extraordinary distance by the intensity of her thought and desire, it is clear that Anne Donne's dead baby cannot have felt a similar urge to be with its unknown and faraway father. Yet it is surely true that Anne Donne's wish to be with her husband at that awful time was not for herself alone, but also for the ill-fated child of their love. She understandably wanted to give him a brief look at the dead infant, which he otherwise would not have had, and in this she was successful. Moreover, if her desire was sufficient to project its wraith along with her own double, this naturally means that a baby acquires its double form sometime prior to its birth, as the Egyptians believed, even though it is destined to be born dead.

These cases make it plain that there is no discernible difference between the double and the wraith, except insofar as they respectively originate from someone who is healthily alive and from someone who is dying or recently dead. But whether either is identical to the ghost is a moot point. Ghosts are of course popularly imagined to have a semi-transparent and hazy appearance, whereas in reality they have, like the double, an outwardly normal appearance. Yet despite their apparent solidity, ghosts are unable to impinge on matter in the same way that the double and the wraith can: they cannot, for example, pick up or otherwise move solid objects, and they are able to pass through otherwise impenetrable barriers like walls and doors with ease. This suggests that they are made of an altogether more tenuous material, if we can call it that. And ghosts rarely, if ever, say anything, which indicates that they lack consciousness.

Not long ago a retired police officer living in Kent described to me the post-death visitation by a wraith to a woman friend belonging to the same Bexley psychic group as himself, whose unexpected appearance shared much in common with that of Wilfred Owen's wraith to his brother.

The lady in question had one day gone into her living room and was astonished to find, sitting in one of the armchairs, the son of a friend of hers. He was staring vacantly into space and paid no attention to her, despite her attempts to get a response from him. In desperation she telephoned the youth's mother, who was most taken aback and upset by her call, as her son, she tearfully revealed, had committed suicide the previous day. Aghast at this, yet scarcely believing it to be true, the woman hurriedly returned to the living room, where she was in time to witness the apparently solid and living young man fade away into nothing. She had absolutely no idea why his wraith had appeared to her, although its purpose may have been, in a somewhat clumsy and confused way, to show her that while suicide is wrong, death is not an end, but a beginning.

The simultaneous appearance of a double and a wraith, like Anne Donne with her dead son, happens but rarely, yet the coming together of two such forms is by no means limited to past times. The following recent case demonstrates that they still happen.

One Saturday morning in 1984, my informant Peter Wood was driving with his mother along the somewhat unusually named Bottoms Lane in Silverdale, Lancashire, when he noticed two elderly gentlemen sitting on a bench at the right side of the road ahead of the car, both of whom he recognized. He was so startled by the sight of them that he pointed them out to his mother, and asked her to describe them to him as they went by. This she did, mentioning in particular the brown trilby hat and glasses worn by one, and the blue felt hat and pebble glasses worn by the other. Her description tallied with what Peter had seen and it convinced him that the figures were an actuality and not a subjective vision, and that the two men were whom he thought they were.

The two old men were in fact brothers and well-known Silverdale residents. Yet the one wearing the blue felt hat, whose name was Fred Burrow, had died ten years previously, while the other, Harvey Burrow, lived in a retirement home. On the following Monday, my bemused correspondent telephoned the retirement home's manager to ask if Harvey had been out on Saturday morning, but was told that Harvey had been asleep in the day-room at the time of the sighting and had not been out all day. This strange fact indicates that it was Harvey's double that the mother and son had spotted sitting with Fred's wraith, both of which looked entirely normal and life-like. But what gives their appearance together an added poignancy is the fact that the elderly and somewhat frail Harvey died the following day, thereby perhaps revealing, as my correspondent suggested, that his brother had come for him. We may also suppose that Harvey's double was stretching its legs, so to speak, in preparation for the great adventure to come.

The frequency with which a person's double is seen at or about the time of his or her death prompted a major investigation into the phenomenon a little over one hundred years ago, which was carried out by Edmund Gurney, F.W.H. Myers, and Frank Podmore, three founder members of the Society for Psychical Research. The several hundred cases they collected, which were sent to them by correspondents from around Great Britain and throughout the Empire, and their explanation of why and how these occurred, were published in 1886 under the title of *Phantasms of the Living*. The book included accounts of not only observed doubles, but also of disembodied voices heard and tactile stimuli felt, that seemingly originated from those about to die, and which explain why the odd word 'phantasms' was used in the title, rather than 'phantoms'.

Unfortunately, however, none of the authors was prepared to accept that doubles might be external, three-dimensional entities, and thus objective in nature, for as one of them put it:

> I scarcely know how far the idea of a literal wraith is seriously entertained by any educated person in the present day. Gaseous and vaporous ghosts are, I imagine, quite at a discount . . . and even if etherial ghosts could be seen, the auditory phenomena would remain a hopeless obstacle to a satisfactory physical explanation of them.

This prejudice resulted in them explaining everything that had been told to them as the product of telepathy.

Thus they would have us believe that a person nearing death and desiring the presence, or thinking longingly about, an absent loved one or a close friend, telepathically sends those desires or thoughts into the visual centres of the absent person's brain, which causes him to create an image of the dying person that is seen as an apparently external figure. Yet what sort of reasoning is it to suppose, for example, that if I as a dying person should longingly wish for the presence of X at my bedside, such thoughts would prompt X to hallucinate an image of me? It makes no sense.

I have suggested that dying people may well be thinking of those to whom their double appears, and *Phantasms of the Living* does present some cases in which a wish to see the individual concerned was expressed to those at the bedside of the dying person. However, in the majority of cases there is no record of what was going on inside the near-departed's head, and without this knowledge we can hardly accept the hypothesis that the doubles that were seen are necessarily telepathically-created illusions. And besides, why should telepathic impulses emanating from the dying act almost exclusively upon the visual centres of the absent one's brain, when in almost every other life circumstance where telepathic contact can be demonstrated, no such stimulation, and the generation thereby of visual hallucinations, is reported?

It is likewise difficult to understand how telepathy could cause the sighting of Fred Burrow's wraith and brother Harvey's double, sitting together in Bottoms Lane, by two witnesses, neither of whom were emotionally close to the men concerned – although the authors of *Phantasms of the Living* would have us believe that in such shared cases, the hallucination is first telepathically engendered in the brain of one, say in this case the son, who then passes it on by similar means to the brain of the other, in this case the mother, who in turn 'projects a kindred image'!

The alternative hypothesis, that doubles actually exist, albeit temporarily in their separated form, does mean that they possess some of the properties at least of the physical people whose likeness they are. Their solidity, for example, must be sufficient to reflect light, so that they can be seen. If they move they must likewise possess some internal power of motion. And if they speak, they must not only have a sufficiently well-organized internal structure to enable them to form and emit audible sound waves, but they must also possess both the intelligence to create spoken words and sufficient of the real individual's personality to reproduce his or her tone and manner. Hence on this basis the double cannot be akin to a hologram, all light and shade without substance, but must rather be a genuine three-dimensional replica, both externally and internally.

In *Supernatural Disappearances* I mention two interesting nineteenth-century cases which suggest that the double has a discernible solidity and thereby an objective existence. One involved Henrietta Piggot-Carleton, whose double was only noticed by her father when it cast a shadow over the page of the book he was reading. She herself was four miles away at the time, sitting on the bank of a river. At the moment of her double's appearance she had noticed that she and her male companion were about to get drenched in a thunderstorm, which she knew would alarm her father and which caused her to wish herself back at home with all her heart.

The other is the famous case of Emilie Sagée, a teacher at an academy in Latvia from 1845–46, whose double was seen on numerous occasions in and around the school by the pupils and by other members of staff, and by the servants. Her double's clarity, interestingly enough, reflected the emotional state of the real woman. 'It was uniformly remarked,' noted the lady who reported the case, 'that the more distinct and material to the sight the double was, the more stiff and languid was the living person; and in proportion as the double faded did the real individual resume her powers.'

On one occasion Emilie Sagée's double appeared in an armchair of a downstairs room when the real person was visible outside picking flowers. It was seen by all forty-two of the girls doing embroidery in the room, two of whom, being somewhat braver than the rest, went up to the seated figure and touched it.

They averred [says my source] that they did feel a slight resistance, which they likened to that which a fabric of fine muslin or crape would offer to the touch. One of the two passed close in front of the armchair, and actually through a portion of the figure. The appearance, however, remained after she had done so, for some time longer, still seated, as before. At last it gradually vanished.

And yet, despite Emilie Sagée's double being regularly and repeatedly seen by the pupils and staff at the school, it was puzzlingly quite invisible to the poor woman herself, who only knew of its presence from the reactions of others! And like Henrietta Piggot-Carleton's double, it did not speak, which suggests that it lacked both cognition and self-awareness.

Similarly, in *Phantasms of the Living* we read of the double of a young woman that appeared to S.J. Masters in 1882. Mr Masters had gone upstairs to bed, lighting his way with a lantern, when he suddenly noticed, standing in the open doorway of his parents' bedroom, the figure of a young woman. He could not, he says, distinguish the dress she wore, but could plainly see her features, especially her eyes. He remained transfixed by the sight of the mysterious intruder for about twenty seconds, when suddenly his mother, having heard him stop on the landing, called to him from below. He noted:

> The figure collapsed when my mother called upstairs, and the light I held in my hand shone through the doorway to the opposite wall, which had been obscured by the figure, as if she had a tangible body.

Mr Masters later discovered that a young woman with whom he had been briefly involved, had died on that same evening. 'I feel convinced it was her,' he adds, 'for the eyes had the same expression, although I could not recognise her at the time; not having seen the girl for quite six months, I had almost forgotten her existence.'

These cases seemingly show that the double is a genuine three-dimensional entity having sufficient 'body' not only to interrupt the passage of light beams but also to reflect them, as normal matter does. But the double is able to do more than simply reflect light. It can also manipulate matter. I shall look at this astonishing property more closely later on.

However, I want to end this chapter by considering two most interesting cases in which a wraith vacates a person's body at the point of death and then goes on to participate in an after death excursion in this world.

The first was described in a work by the Roman writer Varro Terentius (116–28 BC), which has unfortunately been lost, although Pliny the Elder does include an outline of it in his *Natural History*. There is no reason to doubt that the facts of the case as described by Pliny are any different from those given by Terentius.

There once lived in Rome two brothers, both knights, of the family Corfidius, the elder of whom one day collapsed and died. His will disclosed that he had left all his wealth to his brother, who quickly set about organizing his funeral. Yet while these arrangements were being carried out, the deceased brother suddenly, by spontaneous resuscitation, returned to life, and clapped his hands to summon his servants to him. When they gathered fearfully around his death-bed, he told them, to their astonishment, that he – meaning his wraith – had just come back from his brother's house. His sibling, he said, had shown him where he had secretly buried some gold and had begged him to take care of his daughter. Then the younger man went on to add that the funeral arrangements he had made would now be needed for himself. And incredibly, while the elder Corfidius was saying this, some servants of his brother came running in, crying out that the younger man had just fallen down and died. Indeed, when he later went to his brother's house, the older man discovered that the gold was buried at the place which his brother, when alive, had shown to his wraith.

The second story is equally remarkable, although the man whom the wraith meets does not die and is therefore able to personally verify the account of their meeting given by the reanimated man.

Apparently, during the pontificate of Innocent III (1198–1216) a German knight named Everadus Ambula fell sick and likewise seemingly died. Yet some time after he had been laid out, he spontaneously came back to life, and, to the astonishment of those gathered around the bed, he told them that, while dead, his wraith had left his body and had been taken by an 'evil spirit' on an extensive journey, first to Jerusalem and from thence to the camp of Saladin in Egypt. He was next carried off to a wood in the province of Lombardy, where he met and talked with a German friend of his, and then on to Rome, a city he had not visited before, but whose situation, buildings, and the appearance of many of its principal citizens, he was able to describe with exactitude.

Yet although Everadus's accurate depiction of Rome and some of its inhabitants is incredible enough, what is particularly relevant to our study is the fact that the German friend whom he said he encountered in the Lombardy wood, later affirmed that he did indeed meet with Everadus Ambula there, at the very hour and place that he mentioned, that they discussed the very subjects Everadus said they did, and that he was, moreover, quite convinced that he was talking to the real knight!

Hence you can be in two places at the same time, and when your double or wraith is encountered it is indistinguishable from your physical self.

3 Doubles of Sleep and Dreaming

Here in this other world, they come and go
With easy dream-like movements to and fro.
They stare through lovely eyes, yet do not seek
An answering gaze, or that a man should speak.
From *Unknown Country* by Harold Monro

As we have seen, the approach of death, or death itself, often gives rise to, or causes the projection of, the double or wraith of the person concerned. And while this is prompted by him thinking about the individual(s) to whom his double appears, it is none the less brought into being by the loosening of whatever bonds hold the double within the living physical body.

Such bond loosening, if we may call it that, also takes place when we are asleep, which explains why, according to tradition, the doubles of those who are soon to die arrive at a church door at midnight, when the real people are of course slumbering in their beds. There is likewise an increased tendency for doubles to wander abroad when their owner is in a religious or hypnotic trance, or has attained a state of ecstasy, or has fallen into a lethargy or trance. These altered states of consciousness form part of that broad spectrum of mental life, along with others like frenzy, catalepsy and coma, that stretch between ordinary wakefulness and death, although the first is far from being a steady state itself.

But if sleep can prompt the release or the projection of a

double, then it is the emergence from sleep of the person who sees it that often forms the other half of the equation, for the perceptions are seemingly heightened then. This suggests that, in such cases, a genuine two-way interaction goes on. If so, it may mean that our nights are crowded with doubles, although most go completely unnoticed because the fully awake are blind to them and those asleep are unaware of them. And as most wandering doubles seemingly lack self-awareness, they produce no memory within the person's consciousness of their excursions.

The following personal accounts are perhaps typical of the circumstances in which many doubles of sleep manifest, although I had no idea that my double was walking about the house on either occasion.

At seven o'clock in the morning of Tuesday, 18 June 1996, my elderly mother was at home lying asleep in her bed, facing towards the bedroom wall. She suddenly woke up, and turned to see me, as she thought, standing just inside her room, looking around the door at her. She didn't see my face clearly, but was more aware of my tall form and in particular my red dressing gown. She uttered an exclamation of surprise, but I didn't answer her; I instead withdrew silently from the room as she looked at me and closed the door, or so it seemed, behind me. She remained awake for several minutes before going back to sleep again, supposing that she must have dreamt seeing me. I was certainly asleep at the time of my apparent visit, and I didn't wake that morning until about eight o'clock. I have never been known to walk in my sleep. This suggests that my mother saw my double. Yet I had no knowledge of the event until she told me about it at breakfast time. Because my mother was suffering from an injured knee then, which she sustained in a fall, my anxiety about her may have been the reason for my double's unexpected visit.

My double made another appearance to my mother by looking around her bedroom door almost exactly one year later, on 2 June 1997, at 7.45 a.m. This time she was lying awake in bed with her eyes open and was facing towards the door, waiting to get up. Suddenly, she says, she saw the door open and my head appear around it. I looked at her as if to determine that she was all right, and then, evidently deciding that she was, I withdrew my head and closed the door. I said nothing to her, and my visit lasted no more than three or four seconds. As only my head appeared around the door, she could not see what I was wearing. Again, I looked entirely normal and there was no noticeable paleness of my complexion. However, I was then in bed and still asleep, and as before I knew nothing about the occurrence until my mother asked me at breakfast if I had looked in on her before she got up. I hadn't but it seems my double had. Again, some anxiety about my mother's welfare seemingly prompted the out-of-body visit as I had woken earlier at about 5 a.m., when I had felt concerned about her.

A Hereford woman named Sheila recently told me that, early one morning in 1987, her mother had woken to find her apparently standing fully-dressed beside her bed, looking down at her. The two women lived together and occupied adjacent bedrooms. Sheila's mother was startled to see her there and asked her if everything was all right, but received no reply. Instead, the figure turned and noiselessly left the room. Wondering what was the matter, her mother got out of bed and went into Sheila's bedroom, only to find that she was actually fast asleep in bed, clad in her nightie. Thus she hadn't seen her real daughter, but rather her double.

Sheila's double and my own only differed in what they were wearing. For its first visit, my double clad itself in an ersatz dressing gown, while Sheila's opted for reproductions of her daytime clothes. It is difficult to know why Sheila's double did that, unless it had plans to go further afield. However, we both shared what might be the cause of our doubles' appearances; Sheila, like myself, was anxious about her mother, who had been unwell.

Intriguingly, the double of a young girl that appeared to her father, in a case collected and quoted by researchers Celia Green and Charles McCreery, was dressed in pyjamas, like the real child, although they were different from the ones she was wearing at the time!

The incident happened one dark morning in the winter of 1965/6, when the man concerned, a school housemaster, was woken by his alarm clock at 6.45 a.m. He opened his eyes to see, as he thought, his youngest daughter, then four years old, standing beside the bed looking at him with some bewilderment, 'as if unsure of herself'. He was surprised to find her there, yet not unduly startled, as she did, like all young children, occasionally wander into her parents' bedroom during the night or early morning, if she was at all upset or distressed. He was more surprised by the fact that he could clearly see her, despite the room being completely dark, and because she was wearing white, perfectly-fitting pyjamas, whereas her overall tone was a grey misty colour.

The man rose quickly and stepped across to the mantelshelf to turn off the alarm clock, saying 'Hello darling' to his daughter as he did so. Yet when he turned back, she was no longer there. He assumed she must have darted out of the room in the second or two that he looked away, yet he was puzzled by the fact that the bedroom door, which had a loud squeak when opened, had made no sound. So he went immediately into his daughter's next-door bedroom, which she shared with her two sisters, and found, to his astonishment, that not only was the girl fast asleep in bed, but she was clad in an odd pair of pyjamas, the top being yellow, the bottoms red in colour, that were too small for her!

Thus it seems that the girl herself had not gone into her parents' bedroom, but rather her double had. We can only guess why. It may be that the child did not much like wearing her uncomfortable, ill–fitting, odd–coloured pyjamas and had dreamed that she was dressed instead in some comfortable white ones. Then she went to show her daddy how she looked, although she could obviously only do this in her double form, which is perhaps why she felt somewhat unsure of herself. As we shall see later, dreams of the sleeping mind are as often as not the reality experienced by the wandering double.

61

Yet the sceptic, after having examined the possibility of somnambulism (which is possible in my case), will assume rather that a waking dream, or what the French call a *vision hypnogogique*, must be responsible for the likenesses seen. By this is meant a dream of the sleeper that is carried into wakefulness, which causes a dream figure or scene to be seen, when the eyes are opened, as a seemingly external representation that is mistaken for the real thing. This explanation likewise dismisses the double as an objective phenomenon, with no reality outside the viewer's mind. It is a neat, psychological solution to an otherwise intangible problem.

Now my mother did explain my presence the first time by assuming she must have dreamt seeing me, although she was quite sure that she had opened her eyes and looked into the room. She also went straight back to sleep afterwards, which suggests an incomplete awakening. Yet such an assumption is hardly surprising, for how else would most people explain such an odd, one-off phenomenon in the circumstances? However, on the second occasion she was fully awake with her eyes open when my double looked around her door.

And while both the Hereford woman and the school housemaster woke to see their daughters apparently standing by their beds, neither went back to sleep; both in fact followed, as they thought, their offspring out of the room. They knew therefore that the room itself was real, not a dream image. And it makes no sense to suppose that either daughter's likeness somehow became detached, in their minds, from its dream background and then was seemingly transposed, like a cardboard cut-out, at their awakening, to their bedside. But then, neither had been dreaming about their child before they woke up!

Dennis Bardens, the author of biographies of Winston Churchill, Norman Birkett and Princess Margaret, as well as books with a paranormal theme, recently told me that his *doppelgänger* was seen by his wife when they were on their honeymoon, which the young couple spent in a remote Cornish cottage standing between Liskeard and Callington.

One night after they had both gone to sleep, his new bride suddenly woke up to find his double standing by the bed staring down at his sleeping form. Dennis said she could clearly see the figure in the darkened room, because it was somewhat illuminated by an inner light, just as my Montreal girlfriend's double had seemingly been. As the frightened Mrs Bardens shook her husband from the arms of Somnus, the double disappeared, leaving her to explain as best she could why she had so abruptly roused him. After listening to her tale, the chagrined and disbelieving young author snapped, 'What are you complaining about? You've got two for the price of one.'

It is relevant to mention here two women of former times who were surprised by a double when they were lying in their beds.

John Aubrey, for example, reports that the Countess of Thanet one night saw, in the light of a candle burning in her London bedchamber, the double of her daughter, Lady Hatton, who was then some 100 miles distant at Horton in Northamptonshire, where she was doubtless lying asleep in bed. The appearance of Lady Hatton to her mother was a forerunner of the daughter's tragic death, as not long afterwards, in 1675, the poor woman was blown to pieces at her castle in Guernsey, when some gunpowder was ignited by a stroke of lightning.

Similarly, but less ominously, one night in December 1885, following the placement of an old servant named Caroline with a lady living in Croydon, the other servant at the Folkestone house where she had worked, named Elizabeth, was woken by the sound of her bedroom door opening, and saw 'Caroline walk into the room clad in her nightgown, looking very white and wretched'. The startled Elizabeth, thinking it was the real woman, asked her if she wasn't happy in her new home, and commented how worried she looked. However, Caroline's double, for such it was, did not reply, but simply turned from her and left the room, closing the door behind it. On informing her mistress about the incident in the morning, Elizabeth discovered that she (her mistress)

had just received a letter from Caroline, who described in it
how much she disliked her new situation. Thus by temporarily returning to her old home, Caroline's double had done
what her unhappy real self was unable to do, even though, as
later inquiries revealed, she had neither thought about, nor
dreamed of, Elizabeth that night.

Equally puzzling is the experience that Ken Harrison, a
Hastings man, had in January 1996, for although he did not
see the double of his wife, he certainly heard movements suggestive of its presence. Ken has had several hip operations,
which have crippled him, and the pain he still suffers often
keeps him awake at night. He and his wife Joyce live in a bungalow and occupy separate bedrooms.

Late on the night in question Ken heard Joyce's bedroom
door open and her footsteps, or so he thought, go across the
hall into the kitchen. Then he heard the sound of the kettle
being filled and afterwards its lid put on, and the click of the
kettle being switched on (the plug is on the other side of the
wall near the head of Ken's bed). He continued to hear footsteps moving about and thought, 'Oh! Joyce is making a cup
of tea, I expect she'll bring me one.' But after waiting for
some time without anything further happening, Ken wondered if he had been mistaken about Joyce and that instead
an intruder had entered the bungalow. So he felt for his
crutches and with difficulty got out of bed and went into the
hall. He was surprised to find there was no light on anywhere. He first switched on the hall light, and then went into
the kitchen, where he discovered that nothing was out of
place (although unfortunately he neither looked in nor
touched the kettle). Going from there to his wife's bedroom,
he opened the door and saw to his astonishment that she was
sound asleep in bed. 'But I heard it all just as I have told you,'
he said. 'And I wasn't dreaming. What is the explanation?'

What indeed? Was Joyce's double wandering about on its
own, doing what the real Joyce might have done had she been
awake? As no other explanation can seemingly account for
Ken's experience, and given that their bungalow is not haunt-

ed, it looks as if it might have been! But further, if a double has sufficient strength and cohesion to lift a kettle and to turn a tap on, not to mention operate an electrical switch, then it can hardly be a vaporous phantom. Rather, it must be quasi-physical, thereby perhaps belonging to both this world and the next.

When the double appears at a distant place it is somehow projected directly to that spot, thereby materializing out of thin air. Occasionally, however, it is seen to rise from a person's body, just as if the real individual was standing up, and this usually happens when the double does not afterwards go far, as within the confines of its own home. Such a direct uprising of the double was witnessed one night by a woman after her husband had returned home late from a drinking session. Her experience is also recounted by Celia Green and Charles McCreery, in their book entitled *Apparitions*. The husband clumsily woke his wife on entering their bedroom and she remained awake, feeling rather annoyed, for some time afterwards, when she suddenly felt movement on his side of the bed, as if he was getting up.

I lifted my head, and saw him rising swiftly to nearly full height, but slightly bent at the waist, as if ready to run, which he was doing. I sat up startled, and put out a hand to stop him, thinking, by this time, that he was sleep-walking, then suddenly realised that I was leaning on him. He was still in bed, fast asleep, and breathing so quietly that I had to bend down to hear him. He didn't waken in spite of being leaned on . . . It was very odd, because I could see his whole figure in the moonlight, looking solid and normal – in pyjamas.

The reverse of this process, whereby a person who is aware of being out of his body recalls his return into it, was experienced by a young woman early in January 1890. That night, after having gone to bed and fallen asleep, the woman suddenly found herself downstairs in the hall, wondering what on earth she was doing there. She could see everything around her quite clearly, despite the house being in darkness, and noticed that the front door was securely locked. She went quickly and quietly back upstairs, not wanting to wake either the friend who was staying overnight in the same bed as herself or the dog sleeping in its basket.

> She came up noiselessly [her sister-in-law recounted], saw to her relief that the dog had not heard her, looked to the bed where her friend was lying fast asleep, *and*, beside her, saw, to her amazement, her own sleeping body! The sight gave her no sense of alarm, but simply quickened her desire to get back inside that body, which with all despatch she did. This process she can only describe as *dissolving or melting into* her body. The next morning she told her novel experience to her friend, who, of course, thought it an interesting dream; but the *dreamer* is still quite sure she was not asleep, but as much awake as in daily life.

And bizarrely, a Philadelphia woman once divorced her husband because his double had the habit of appearing in their bedroom, if a report appearing in the Philadelphia *Mirror* of 1889 can be believed. Margaret Clements dearly loved her husband Anson, but:

> it had repeatedly occurred that she would be awakened in the night to find a person who looked precisely like [him] moving about the room and sometimes shaving himself directly in front of the bureau while the body of her husband lay beside her as cold as ice, stiff as a corpse, and in a condition that he could not be awakened.

Yet when the frightened Mrs Clements at last managed to shake her husband awake, his double faded and vanished, but its constant appearance in their bedroom was too much for her nerves, and upon finding that her husband had no control over its nocturnal activities, despite being aware of them – 'It has been,' Anson told her, 'the curse of my existence for years, and seems to be a visitation upon me for some sin of my parents,' – she decided their marriage had to end. She regretfully told the divorce court judge:

> Now, sir, you can readily see that no matter how much Anson and I love each other we cannot live as man and wife when this shadow, or whatever you call it, goes roaming around the house at midnight, and so we have concluded to separate.

I cannot vouch for the truth of this story, but if the divorce was improperly instituted by Margaret Clements on these grounds, her 'choice of means', to borrow and paraphrase a quote from the well-known American writer Ambrose Bierce, 'is certainly one of the most amazing ever made by a sane human being'.

If sleep more readily allows the separation of the double from the body, as the above examples suggest, this process may be enhanced by the drinking of alcohol. On the evening when I was consciously able to separate myself from my body, for example, I had previously drunk a couple of bottles of brown ale, which served to relax me if nothing else, while the husband mentioned earlier had clearly partaken even more generously of the cup that cheers.

A most interesting personal account of a drink-associated double separation was sent to me by John S., who lives at Maidenhead in Berkshire, and which happened to him following a carousal in London in 1975. One Saturday morning he travelled to the capital to meet friends who owned a shop in the Portobello Road, and when the shop closed they all went out for a drink together. John said:

> It was a bit selfish of me as I hadn't bothered to telephone my fiancée in Maidenhead, and as the evening drew on I [became] more and more intoxicated. By

9.30 p.m. we all went back to my friends' house in Crouch Hill as I couldn't make it safely home. My friends threw a load of scatter cushions down on the living room floor, and I slumped on to them and instantly fell into a deep sleep.

John S. awoke the following morning feeling pretty wretched and eventually set off back to Maidenhead at around 11 a.m. When he arrived home he telephoned his fiancée, who was very short with him, and told her that he would call to see her at about four o'clock that afternoon.

On going to her house, however, John was presented with his fiancée's 'very sour looking' face, which told him she wasn't at all pleased to see him.

She was even more incensed when I apologized for not letting her know I'd stayed in London all night. In fact she called me a liar. She had passed me, she said, around 10 p.m. that Saturday night in her car, in her road. She had her brother with her as a passenger. She sounded the horn and stopped. I stood on the kerb staring at her car. She reversed back to where I was standing, opened the door and asked if I wanted a lift and to get in. Again I just stood and glared at them without uttering a word, at which they slammed the door and drove off leaving me standing on the kerb glaring.

As might be expected, this led to a heated argument between the two, with John loudly protesting that he hadn't been in Maidenhead then, while his fiancée equally vehemently insisted that he had. During the row the woman's brother came in and, to John's surprise, asked him with a sneer, 'What was up with you last night?' The poor man came in for more abuse when he replied that he had spent the night in London.

I was now becoming very concerned. Her brother insisted I was only about five feet from him when he opened the passenger door and said 'Get in', and I had known them both extremely well for the past seven years. They had no doubt at all that they'd seen me that Saturday night in Maidenhead, they are not given to flights of fancy, me neither. But there was no doubt that I was comatose on a floor in North London then.

Maidenhead is about 28 miles as the crow flies from Crouch End, which suggests that John's double was directly projected there while he was wrapped in intoxicated sleep. His lack of awareness of his double's departure or of it standing forlornly on a street in Maidenhead, presumably either means that his consciousness did not travel with the double or that his memory was impaired by the alcohol he had drunk. His double's glaring, zombie-like attitude is not uncommon, as we have seen, and is suggestive of the former. We can perhaps identify a reason for its journey to Maidenhead in the sense of guilt that John felt when he slumped down on the floor of his friends' flat. He wanted to let his fiancée know that he wasn't coming home, and because he couldn't physically accomplish that, in the circumstances, his double tried its best to get the message across to her. It was a pity that it only made things worse for him, not better.

Yet in places like Tibet, where the double is accepted for what it is, that is, as a second self, it can play a useful social role, by being sent ahead, for example, to alert a host of the imminent arrival of his expected guests, or at moments of grave personal danger it may save the real person's life by leading the pursuers one way, while he runs to safety in another. This use of the double may be a spontaneous happening, or for those adepts who learn to control and direct its movements, it may be willed.

Yet if sleep, with or without alcohol, more readily allows the separation of the double, then when the consciousness leaves with it, its experiences will typically be viewed by the sleeping person as a dream. It is a matter of debate whether all dreams represent the movement of the conscious double into the outer world (or even into other realms of being), or if most are fantasies created within our minds. Yet there is growing evidence that when someone dreams he is moving about in what we call the real world, the images are being seen through the eyes of the separated double. Hence it is not a dream as such, but rather direct viewing. This concept is expressed in the following lines from a poem by John Masefield:

> *I fell into a dream and walked apart*
> *Into the night (I thought), into the swart,*
> *Thin, lightless air in which the planet rides;*
> *I trod on dark air upward with swift strides.*

An interesting example of how such direct viewing is confused with a dream is recorded in *Phantasms of the Living.* One night in June 1883, Constance Bevan had an apparent dream about her friend Miss Elliot, who was staying with her, and which began by her being told that Miss Elliot was dead.

> I instantly, in my dream, rushed to her room, entered it, went to her bedside and pulled the clothes from off her face. She was quite cold; her eyes were wide open and staring at the ceiling. This so frightened me that I dropped at the foot of her bed, and knew no more about it until I was half out of bed in my own room and wide awake. The time was 5 o'clock a.m.

But while that was Constance's dream, or so she thought, Miss Elliot, who was lying awake in bed at the time, heard Constance come into the room and felt her do those very things. She reports:

> I awoke on the morning of June 10th, and was lying on my back with my eyes fixed on the ceiling, when I heard the door open and felt someone come in and bend over me, but not far enough to come between my eyes and

the ceiling; knowing it was only C[onstance], I did not move, but instead of kissing me she suddenly drew back, and going towards the foot of the bed, crouched down there . . . Upon this a sort of horror came over me, and I dared not look toward the figure . . . [Then] she touched my foot, and a cold chill ran through me and I knew nothing more till I found myself out of bed looking for C[onstance], who must, I felt, be still in the room. I never doubted that she had really been there until I saw both doors fastened on the inside. On looking at my watch it was a few minutes past 5.

It is important to note that despite Miss Elliot apparently hearing a door of her bedroom open, Constance Bevan could not have entered it by sleep-walking there, or by stealing in there unannounced, as both doors of the room were locked from the inside. Hence she was not physically in Miss Elliot's bedroom. The incident, however, certainly began as a dream, in which Constance was told that her friend was dead, and that this alarming announcement prompted her double to project into Miss Elliot's bedroom, where it anxiously examined the 'dead' woman in the way that not only she but Miss Elliot also experienced, as well as performing the other stated actions.

Such external double activity during the course of an apparent dream is implicit in Thomas Hood's famous poem *The Dream of Eugene Aram*, wherein he presents Aram, a school usher at Lynn, in Norfolk, telling one of the schoolboys about how murderers are pursued by the ghosts of their victims:

> *And well, quoth he, I know, for truth*
> *Their pangs must be extreme, –*
> *Woe, woe, unutterable woe –*
> *Who spill life's sacred stream!*
> *For why? Methought, last night, I wrought*
> *A murder in a dream.*

71

And after the dream murder was done, Aram recalls in horror how he was unable to get rid of the victim's body, as neither water nor earth would keep it covered over and thus out of sight.

> *O God! that horrid, horrid dream*
> *Besets me now awake!*
> *Again – again, with dizzy brain,*
> *The human life I take;*
> *And my red right hand grows raging hot,*
> *Like Cranmer's at the stake.*

Yet while this was apparently only the stuff of a nightmare, the man in it had actually been murdered, which led to the arrest of Aram:

> *That very night, while gentle sleep*
> *The urchin eyelids kiss'd,*
> *Two stern-faced men set out from Lynn,*
> *Through the cold and heavy mist;*
> *And Eugene Aram walk'd between,*
> *With gyves upon his wrist.*

The reality behind the poem is less colourful, yet Eugene Aram was a self-educated polymath and linguist, who conducted his own defence at his trial for the murder of Daniel Clark, a Knaresborough shoemaker, of which he was found guilty although the evidence against him was largely circumstantial. Aram was hanged at York (where his trial had also taken place) on 6 August 1759.

The classic account of how the apparent dream of one individual was the reality of another, who saw the person concerned in his double form, happened in 1754. It is worth repeating not only because it is true, but because it likewise suggests that dreams may well take us out of ourselves, some into this world and some into alternative realities, which may either be pleasant or extremely unpleasant (as in nightmares).

Doubles of Sleep and Dreaming

One night a 23-year-old theological student named Joseph Wilkins, who attended an academy in Devonshire, dreamed that he was making a journey to London. He then decided he would take the opportunity to visit his parents, who lived in Gloucestershire, about one hundred miles away. When he arrived in his dream at his parents' house, he first tried to get in through the front door, but finding it locked went around to the back door, through which he successfully gained entry. He next climbed the stairs to his parents' bedroom.

When he entered the room, he first went to the bed where his father was; whom he found asleep: on which, without disturbing him, he went round to the other side of the bed, where he found his mother, as he apprehended, broad awake: to whom he addressed himself, in these words: 'Mother! I am going on a long journey, and am come to bid you goodbye.' On which, she answered in a fright, as follows: 'O dear son, thou art dead!'

At that moment Joseph Wilkins woke up and assumed he had simply had a somewhat odd dream. Yet to his astonishment a few days afterwards he received a letter from his father, who told him that on that same night his mother had heard someone, having first unsuccessfully tried to open the front door, come in at the back of the house and climb the stairs. She had then been alarmed to see him (Joseph) enter their bedroom and speak to her as follows: 'Mother! I am going on a long journey, and am come to bid you goodbye.' To which, thinking it was his wraith that addressed her, she answered: 'O dear son, thou art dead!' His double then disappeared, and the terrified woman woke her husband and told him what had happened, insisting that she was fully awake and had not dreamed what she said.

One hundred years later, on 19 May 1854, a Toronto man named E.V. Wilson had a very similar experience. That Friday afternoon he dozed off at his desk at home and dreamed he was in Hamilton, a city lying forty miles west of Toronto. In

73

the dream he first completed some business, then he stopped to make a friendly call on a lady named Mrs D——s. He rang her doorbell, but was disappointed to learn from the servant who answered the door that Mrs D——s was out and would be away for about one hour. Mr Wilson therefore left his name and asked that his compliments be given to the lady, and went on his way. It was at that point that he woke up and put the dream out of his mind.

But then a few days later a letter from Mrs D——s was received by a female member of Mr Wilson's household, in which the writer, among other matters, mentioned that she was sorry to have missed seeing Mr Wilson when he called that day, and added that she had afterwards vainly visited all of Hamilton's hotels in the expectation of catching him before he left the city.

Mr Wilson was completely nonplussed by this, knowing as he did that while he had dreamed of being in Hamilton, he had not visited the city for over a month. But having had his interest aroused, he organized a party of friends to go with him to Hamilton, with the express intention of calling upon Mrs D——s. Having apprised Mrs D——s of his plan, the lady herself answered the door when Mr Wilson's group arrived, and on ushering them into the living room, she then asked her servants to go among her guests and attend to their needs, and to take particular note if there was anyone they recognized. Mr Wilson was even more astonished when two of the servants instantly identified him as the man who had called there ten days previously and who had left his name, which they correctly repeated to Mrs D——s.

And likewise, in John Aubrey's *Miscellanies* we read of how a Monsieur Periesk, who had never been to London, once dreamed, as he thought, that he was in the English capital walking down a broad thoroughfare, when he came to a goldsmith's shop, which he entered and admired a handsome antique Otho coin (presumably a Roman coin minted during the three-month reign of Emperor Marcus Salvius Otho in AD 69) in a glass desk. Then when Monsieur Periesk actually visited London, he one day walked in Cheapside (as Aubrey believed) and came across the shop he had 'dreamed' about, recognized the goldsmith's features, and on entering the shop found to his absolute astonishment the coin he had admired in an identical glass desk!

Aubrey does not record the effect that such a startling correspondence of dream and reality had on Monsieur Periesk, but a similar encounter had a very unsettling influence on the poet Percy Bysshe Shelley. The confrontation with his 'dream' images occurred one day in 1810, when Shelley was out taking a stroll with a friend (probably Thomas Hogg) in the neighbourhood of Oxford, where he was a student. The high banks and hedges of the country lane along which they were walking had prevented them from seeing the surrounding scenery, but then, on turning a corner, a part of it was suddenly revealed. Shelley wrote:

> The view consisted of a windmill standing in one among many plashy meadows, enclosed with stone walls; the irregular and broken ground, between the wall and the road on which we stood; a long low hill behind the windmill, and a grey covering of uniform cloud spread over the evening sky . . . The scene surely was a common scene . . . The effect which it produced on me was not such as could have been expected. I suddenly remembered to have seen that exact scene in some dream of long –

The poet unexpectedly ended his narrative there, but later appended this note of explanation, 'Here I was obliged to leave off overcome by thrilling horror'. After Shelley's death, his wife Mary described the dramatic effect that his mere recalling of the event that day had had on him: 'I remember well his coming to me from writing it, pale and agitated, to seek refuge in conversation from the fearful emotions it excited'. The dream referred to may of course have been prophetic, yet if that is so the scene it previewed was strangely without consequence. However, it may have been, as I suspect it was, really a view of that particular expanse of Oxfordshire countryside as seen through the eyes of Shelley's wandering double.

Even more intriguing is the notion that if our doubles do leave our bodies in our sleep, then we may actually lead two entirely different sorts of lives, the 'normal' one when we are awake and another or others in our double form when we are asleep. Thus your double may occupy some house and town elsewhere in the country, or even in a foreign place, where it is regarded as a perfectly ordinary, if frequently absent person, to whom you are as much a mystery as it is to you, and who may even have its own family!

This amazing possibility is suggested by the strange dreams of life in another place dreamed by a churchman, which were not only remarkably consistent but were just as real to him as his waking existence. He wrote:

> I do not know whether this or any other writer has observed anything like what happens to me, that this world of our own (in dreams) is as constant and regular in many particulars, as the common waking one. To explain myself, I have rambled for twenty years together in dreams, in one certain country, through one certain road, and resided in one certain country-house, quite different as to the whole face of the country, and situation of the place, from anything I ever saw awake, and the scene quite unvaried.

But while the idea of such a literal double life is intriguing, could it really happen? Has anyone, for example, who has regularly dreamed of visiting or living in a place like that mentioned above ever found it in his or her waking life? Such a discovery would not only mean that the dreamer had been at the place or places concerned in his double form, but it would also explain why *déjà vu* experiences occur.

The answer is yes, several people have. Novelist Fay

Weldon is one of them, and she described her remarkable experience in a recent article in *The Times* (18 February 1997). Indeed, what happened to her is made doubly interesting (no pun intended) by the fact that the 'dream' location in which she found herself formed part of a nightmare. And when she, quite by chance, came across the same place in waking life in her late twenties, her behaviour elicited by the shock of this gave her a fresh insight into herself, which in turn, she claimed, helped prevent the dreaded nightmare from returning.

I'd had a recurring 'bad dream' for years; in which I was making my way up a mountain in a place which looked like Transylvania – certainly vampire country. Night was falling. We – a vague group – stopped at a country inn. I would be given a room off an upper corridor; and go to bed and try to sleep. But moonlit forest branches scrabbled against the window; and eventually claws, too, and the window would crack, and howling, demented creatures spring at me – and I'd wake, and the terror last for hours.

'Then one night,' she continued, 'reality caught up with the dreams.' This occurred when she went on a motoring holiday in Austria with her husband and their young child, and the family nanny. Suddenly, when they drove out of Innsbruck as night was falling:

To my terror, I recognized the road as the one in my dream [she went on]. With every curve the place became more familiar ... We stopped at the first *auberge* we came to – thank God it wasn't at all like the one in the dream. I remember my relief. But then it turned out the inn was full. Staff led us to an annexe – and there the nightmare house stood, in all its gabled, steep-roofed detail. Up the familiar stairs with the carved oak bannisters, along the upstairs corridor, the white-aproned maid showed us our two rooms, facing each other. In the room to the right, moonlit branches scrabbled against the window pane – the one to the left looked out over a valley, calm, benign and still.

Faced with the choice of which room to sleep in, Fay Weldon opted for the one overlooking the valley. She is not proud of herself for this, for it meant that her own child and the nanny had to occupy the one through whose window, in her dreams, the 'demented creatures' sprang at her in the night. No such horror took place, however, and the night passed quietly for all.

And happily, Miss Weldon never had her nightmare again. She assumes this was because she couldn't pretend any longer that she was a wholly good person but was 'as cowardly and self-interested as anyone else' and that she was 'responsible for my own nightmares. They were self-generated'. But we might take issue with her. After all, the repeated nightmare was the experience of her double, and it showed her what would happen to her if she ever slept in that particular room. Hence by avoiding the room, she avoided the terrifying creatures that were waiting to spring at her. They were not lying in wait for anyone else, so there was no danger to her child or nanny. She therefore did the sensible thing. The nightmare was in this sense predictive, and once the moment of danger had passed there was no reason for it to return; it had saved Fay from a horror that might have been fatal to her.

Furthermore, although Fay Weldon's double entered that Austrian *auberge* room on the nights when she was asleep and dreaming, the element of forewarning in the dreams suggests that the second self may not be fixed entirely in the present moment but can perhaps range forwards and backwards in time.

This hypothesis is certainly supported by the dream experience of Peter Ackroyd, who describes (*The Times*, 1 August 1996) how, one night a few weeks previous to that date, he was able to take control of the dream he realized he was having and thereby direct himself into the past. He did this by simply saying he wanted to be taken into the eighteenth century. To his surprise he immediately found himself in an eighteenth century street.

> I remarked to myself that the stone exteriors, the windows and the dress of the people seemed absolutely authentic. It was, to be specific, the early 18th century. At one point I remembered being informed that I was in Hendon. I asked to be taken to the pesthouse or hospital – at which point someone laughed, and said that they were the same thing. There the pesthouse was before me. I entered it, but the stench was so strong that I retched and rushed outside. There the dream ended.

It must be emphasized that it wasn't Peter Ackroyd's consciousness which was floating unobserved around this past scene, but rather his visible double that was walking about and talking with the inhabitants. He of course felt entirely as if he were there in his normal form, which in a sense he was, except that it wasn't his physical self that his consciousness was occupying but his double or second self.

Moreover, Mr Ackroyd didn't wake up when the eighteenth century scene vanished but returned instead to his former dream state, which he again recognized, and not wishing to end his ramblings in time, he immediately expressed a wish to be taken to 1858. He continues:

> A door appeared before me. I opened it and I was within a mid-Victorian interior where the carpeting and furnishings were, to my eye, quite genuine. I walked into another room, and found it to be a study. The items upon the desk, and the furniture, were again right in detail and general effect. A woman came into the room who seemed to know me very well.

Hence instead of being regarded as an unwanted intruder, the woman greeted him like a member of the family – and then enquired why he was back so early! On replying that he needed some air, the woman went with him down a staircase, and when he asked her to describe where she lived, she said it was in Kensington, West London.

I left the house and there, to my astonishment (and, I must say, slight unease) was a street of the mid-19th century, with the doors, façades and areas exactly as they once had been. My dream ended rather abruptly when a late 20th-century London taxi pulled up.

The past he entered, Ackroyd comments, was so palpably real that he feared he 'might never be able to leave it'. Yet its very authenticity suggests that it wasn't a mental construct or fantasy, and Ackroyd admits that he simply doesn't have the knowledge of either the early eighteenth century or the mid-nineteenth century to create such historically accurate dream scenarios. This may therefore mean that he actually travelled through time in his double form, which in itself suggests, as I have argued in my forthcoming book *A Brief History of Time Travel*, that time is a continuum, and that although our physical self remains trapped in a sliding instant we call 'the present', our double or second self, when we are asleep, is able to explore this continuum at will.

4 The Waking Double

And on the north within the ring,
Appear'd the form of England's King,
Who then, a thousand leagues afar,
In Palestine waged holy war:
From *Marmion* by Sir Walter Scott

The waking double – by which I mean the double that has originated from someone who is awake – is considered in both this chapter and the next, although here I will examine those cases where the double of someone who is awake is seen by another, whereas in the following chapter, I shall look at those where the awake person sees his own double, and thus seemingly himself.

As the cases discussed below reveal, a person who is awake can carry on perfectly well without his (or her) double, which suggests that it isn't as necessary to our functioning as conciousness (or the khu) is. In fact it is possible that the double isn't really needed at all until the body dies, when it seemingly departs like an escape vehicle to another realm carrying our consciousness with it. Hence when it separates from us during life it is perhaps doing little more than running through the escape procedure. Indeed, it may even be that the double is our real self, while the body is no more than a temporary receptacle for it, rather like a chrysalis containing a butterfly, and which allows the double to experience life in the physical world, with all its frustrations, hazards, temptations and pain, as well as its occasional joys. If so, I will leave the reader to decide whether this is wholly a learning experience or rather a grotesque punishment for some pre-birth misdeed.

There are many accounts on record of unrecognized figures that have mysteriously appeared and then disappeared. They are usually thought to be ghosts (which is perhaps a reasonable assumption if they were dressed in old-fashioned clothes) or alternatively they are dismissed as being hallucinations, which are created, as William Shenstone claimed, in 'persons after a debauch of liquor, or under the influence of terror, or in the deleria of a fever, or in a fit of lunacy, or even walking in their sleep'. Yet as often as not such enigmatic apparitions are the doubles of living people who are unknown to us. The following personal experience is perhaps typical of such sudden arrivals and departures.

When I was ten years old, I went with my parents to a Devon holiday camp, where I became friends with another boy of about the same age. We went for a country ramble together on our last day there, and as we trudged back along the narrow path that had taken us to a reservoir, I saw a woman ahead walking down the path towards us. She was dressed in an up-to-date polka-dot dress and was accompanied by a small dog on a lead. Then, when she was about twenty yards away, she suddenly turned to her right and went with her dog through what I presumed was a gap in the tall flanking hedge. Yet when my friend and I reached the spot where she had left the path, we found there was no gap in the hedge – and neither was woman or dog visible in the field beyond. They had seemingly vanished into thin air, although my friend, perhaps significantly, had seen neither. But none the less, we both ran back to our parents more scared than we had ever been! I cannot tell if the woman and her dog supernaturally disappeared or if they were the doubles of a living woman and her canine. But I'm quite sure they weren't hallucinations, for why should I have seen such figures on that otherwise happy day and on no other?

Another figure that appeared and vanished in similar circumstances was seen by Mrs Jill Eaton one Sunday afternoon in September 1980, when she was walking her dog along the path connecting the A223 main road with the Westerham Heights end of Newbarn Lane in Kent. Like the path I walked along, this also had tall dense hedges on either side of it with open fields beyond them, and there was nobody else in sight. At one spot Mrs Eaton's dog stopped to sniff at the ground, and after watching him for a moment or two, she looked up, when to her surprise, as she recounted:

I saw, roughly 50ft in front of me, an elderly man, face towards me, dressed in a fly-fronted raincoat and flat cap. He was stationary, hands cupped in front of his face, as if lighting a pipe or cigarette. I looked back at the dog wondering which one of us, the old chap or me, was going to give way to make room for the other to pass on such a narrow path. The dog being ready to continue his walk, we started forward again – but the man was gone. He had completely vanished as quickly as he had appeared.

Jill Eaton also examined the hedges for any sign of a gap, but found none at all, not even an aperture sufficiently large for a cat or small dog to get through. But when she arrived at the place where the man had stood:

the dog, apparently having been totally unaware of the man a minute or so beforehand, froze to the ground, the hair stood up on the back of his neck and I could not get him to shift for several seconds before he decided to push on. I also noticed a slightly pungent smell of tobacco smoke in the air.

Trying to explain what had happened, Mrs Eaton asks: 'Could it have been what the Germans call a *doppelgänger*, I wonder? Someone who loved that footpath or general area and imagined himself to be there at that particular time. It must have been a supernatural appearance, and disappearance as well.'

I can't of course unequivocally say that the old man was someone's double, although he may well have been. However, when Mrs Eaton later described the elderly man's appearance to her sister-in-law, the latter thought it sounded as if it was her father, who had died in 1970 and who had loved to walk along the path when he was alive – although Mrs Eaton didn't recognize him as her father-in-law. But if it was, then Mrs Eaton probably saw his wraith, the double-form surviving after death, rather than his ghost. It seems doubtful that Mrs Eaton would have hallucinated an unrecognized figure on that otherwise perfectly ordinary, stress-free walk. Besides, how can we explain the reaction of her dog if she had?

The difficulty of determining whether a double (or a wraith) is truly external to us or is instead a subjective vision, is nicely pointed up by an old, but none the less very interesting case, which has considerable relevance to the practicality, if I may call it that, of phantom image generation by the brain's visual centres.

Towards the end of the eighteenth century a Berlin author and bookseller named Christoph Friedrich Nicolai (1733–1811) began seeing doubles of people, some of whom he recognized, some not. He had been suffering from a rather vaguely defined 'congestion of the head' for several years, which might at first be thought responsible for the mysterious figures he saw, although they did not make their appearances until early in 1791, when Christoph Nicolai was, as he says:

much affected in my mind by several incidents of a very disagreeable nature; and on the 24th of February a circumstance occurred which irritated me extremely. At ten o'clock in the forenoon my wife and another person came to console me; I was in a violent perturbation of mind, owing to a series of incidents which had altogether wounded my moral feelings, and from which I saw no possibility of relief: when suddenly I observed at the distance of ten paces from me a figure – the figure of a deceased person. I pointed at it, and asked my wife whether she did not see it. She saw nothing, but being alarmed endeavoured to compose me, and sent for a physician. The figure remained some seven or eight minutes, and at length I became a little more calm.

Later that day, at about four o'clock in the afternoon, Herr Nicolai was again terrified by a second appearance of the same apparition. And when he hurriedly went into the room where his wife was to tell her about it, the figure manifested in there, although it was still quite invisible to her. He noted:

Sometimes it was present, sometimes it vanished; but it was always the same standing figure. A little after six o'clock several stalking figures appeared; but they had no connection with the standing figure. I can assign no other reason for this apparition than that, though much more composed in my mind, I had not been able so soon entirely to forget the cause of such deep and distressing vexation, and had reflected on the consequences of it, in order, if possible, to avoid them.

This ghost or hallucination never appeared again, although Christoph Nicolai did see other figures not long afterwards, some of which he knew, some he didn't know, and among the former were likenesses of both the living, which predominated, and the dead. He also noticed that he never saw the doubles of people with whom he conversed regularly, but only those who lived at some distance away.

They did not always continue present – they frequently left me altogether, and again appeared for a short or longer space of time, singly or more at once; but, in general, several appeared together. For the most part I saw human figures of both sexes; they commonly passed to and fro as if they had no connection with each other, like people at a fair where all is bustle; sometimes they appeared to have business with one another. Once or twice I saw amongst them persons on horseback, and dogs and birds; these figures all appeared to me in their natural size, as distinctly as if they had existed in real life, with the several tints on the uncovered parts of the body, and with all the different kinds of colours of clothes. But I think, however, that the colours were somewhat *paler* than they are in nature.

The next interesting development happened about a month after the appearance of the first figure, when the likenesses, which had previously been silent, began speaking.

Sometimes the phantoms spoke with one another; but for the most part they addressed themselves to me; those speeches were in general short, and never contained anything disagreeable. Intelligent and respected friends often appeared to me, who endeavoured to console me in my grief, which still left deep traces in my mind. This speaking I heard most frequently when I was alone; though sometimes I heard it in company, intermixed with the conversation of real persons; frequently in single phrases only, but sometimes in connected discourse.

Thus described, the figures seen by Christoph Nicolai share many of the characteristics of doubles that I have already mentioned. They were, for example, completely life-like and ordinary in appearance and size, yet somewhat paler in colouring. Many were of persons well known to him, and these tried to comfort him in his state of anxiety and upset. This is hardly surprising, for we have likewise discovered that when someone is worried or concerned about another or has a desire to be with him, then his double is far more likely to appear to him.

But what is particularly noteworthy about these surprising

manifestations, and which may help us to decide whether or not they were created in Christoph Nicolai's mind, was his complete failure to generate them at will.

> When these apparitions had continued some weeks [he observes], and I could regard them with the greatest composure, I afterwards endeavoured, at my own pleasure, to call forth phantoms of several acquaintances, whom I for that reason represented to my imagination in the most lively manner, but in vain. – For however accurately I pictured to my mind the figures of such persons, I never once could succeed in my desire of seeing them *externally*.

He also tried to determine if their appearance was linked in some way with his thought processes or activities at the time, but again without finding any causal relationship:

> I very often reflected on my previous thoughts, with a view to discover some law in the association of ideas, by which exactly these or other figures might present themselves to the imagination . . . but, on the whole, I could trace no connection which the various figures that thus appeared and disappeared to my sight had, either with my state of mind or with my employments, and the other thoughts which engaged my attention.

Hence if the figures had no connection with Herr Nicolai's conscious mind, at least as far as he could determine, then it is hardly likely that they sprang from his subconscious, particularly as they were all perfectly ordinary-looking individuals, many of whom he knew, without any of the freakish or even terrible characteristics that are commonly associated with subconscious images. And even though Nicolai convinced himself that they were imaginary, or in other words hallucinations, I beg to differ with him, firstly because the appearance of his figures accords with virtually every other description of doubles, and secondly, because his mental disquiet, rather than generating the facsimiles, was instrumental in sensitizing him to see them. The following personal story will help explain the last point.

Some years ago I suffered a mental trauma that was more intense, I believe, than the one experienced by Christoph Nicolai. It was caused by the sudden and completely unexpected death of my wife. I won't detail my feelings at the time, except to say that her passing was the emotional equivalent to being struck by lightning.

However, my grief and shock did not result in my seeing apparitional figures, but it did enable me to witness something which was, in its own way, just as remarkable. For on the second or third day after her death I suddenly found that I could see, radiating from the centre of my chest, a burst of pale, golden-coloured light, which projected in front of me to a distance of about six or seven inches, and through which I could pass my hands without them in any way interfering with its form or outpouring.

I soon found that I was not the only person who possessed this beautiful light: for on going outdoors I noticed that everybody else now had a similar burst of pale brilliance emanating from their chests, and which seemingly originated from their hearts, like mine, although it was fainter on some people than others. It was an astonishing and wonderful thing to see, and all the more marvellous for its unexpectedness, although I must say that, strange as it may seem, I simply accepted the light as something I had not seen before, such was the trauma of what had previously happened. The light remained visible for about two whole days, for on the third day, as far as I remember, the radiance faded and eventually disappeared from sight. I have never seen the light since, but I have no doubt that it still shines from me, just as it does from you.

Now I don't believe it was an hallucination, which my brain's visual centres somehow created in order to perhaps comfort me at that bleak time; indeed, seeing the light did not lessen my grief in any way. Moreover, I had never, to my recollection, imagined that we humans possess light radiating from our chests, and although I had seen representations of the Sacred Heart giving out a burst of light, it was never an image that held any significance for me, being a Protestant, or which played any part in my thoughts or concerns. Hence it seems highly unlikely that my mind would have selected that particular image to externalize, if it was hallucinatory. Rather, it seems more likely that my distressed mental state spontaneously sensitized me to briefly viewing a real phenomenon which is normally quite invisible to us. And this is surely why Christoph Nicolai's figures became visible to him, his mental disquiet providing the means by which he was able to see and later to hear the otherwise invisible and inaudible doubles of people, many of whom were his friends and who were concerned about him.

The stress of an upsetting life experience, like a divorce, a change of job or of residence, or an accident or an illness, may also prompt the projection of someone's double in a seemingly random and purposeless way, as the following example illustrates.

In the early summer of 1963 Lily Stenton, then a girl of seventeen years old, left her home in Sheffield to work at a petrol station at Woodford Bridge in Essex. It was a big step for her, with all its attendant uncertainties and excitements, and although Lily enjoyed her work, she soon found that the petrol fumes gave her very bad nose bleeds, which made her anaemic and caused her to faint on several occasions. It was during this difficult period, much to Lily's surprise, that she learned her double had apparently been seen. She told me:

When I had been there a few weeks, I went to work one day and several regular customers came in throughout the day and said they had seen me the day before in a part of Essex that I wasn't even familiar with and had never been to. Apparently I was on a road in the middle of nowhere but for different reasons none of these people stopped to speak to me or offered me a lift, even though some of them seemed to be quite worried about me and were glad to see that I was all right.

Her likeness had been observed, Lily added, by five or six different sets of people as they drove past, all of whom said she looked lost or distressed. They also told her that she was standing, like John S.'s double on the kerbside in Maidenhead, beside the North Circular road, about ten miles from the garage where she was working.

I was just extremely surprised the next day when so many people said they had seen me. I just kept saying it wasn't me but I know that some of them didn't believe me. I was happy where I worked and quite pleased with life in general although it was an emotional time.

It is relevant to mention that during the nine months Lily lived in London she had a number of spontaneous out-of-body or astral travel experiences at her flat, and while the first took her into a local cinema, it so frightened her that she remained on subsequent occasions within the confines of her bedroom. Yet she was quite unaware of her double's projection to, and sojourn on, the North Circular road, which suggests that the two types of experience, although similar in some respects, are not the same. I shall discuss this further in a later chapter.

The appearance of a double beside a road, or walking along a road, is frequently reported, just as is its disappearance by either stepping through a gap (whether real or apparent) in a hedge or a wall or by vanishing into thin air.

The double of Tony, who lives in Cleveland, was seen walking beside the same road that he normally walked along to get to work.

When I was working on a certain site [he told me], I walked to work every morning for about eight or nine months. One Saturday morning I was supposed to be at work, but I was actually at home. When I got to work the next day a few of the guys said to me, 'I stopped to give you a lift in the car yesterday but you just ignored me and walked straight on'. I thought at first it was an elaborate wind-up. Now I work for my brother-in-law and we're pretty close. So a couple of months later I said to him, 'Was it a wind-up that day?' and he says, 'Oh no!' 'Cause they even approached him to ask him where I was. I used to wear a combat jacket and blue jeans as my working gear, so they were absolutely certain it was me.

Tony's double, like that of John S., took absolutely no notice of the people who stopped to offer it a lift, which suggests that it also lacked any awareness of where it was and what it was doing. This may also be true of the double of Lily Stenton, although its unhappy appearance may mean that it was aware of its surroundings but could not place where it was or why it was there. If so, her double's mental state, if we may call it that, was probably similar to that of a diabetic with low blood sugar.

Another correspondent whose double was seen behaving vacantly beside a road is Mrs Brenda Collins of Poole in Dorset. She was apparently spotted in Branksome, one mile from her home in Parkstone, by a friend with whom she works. Both are districts of Poole. The incident took place at about 5.15 p.m. one Wednesday in 1987.

When my friend came into work next day, she said, 'I saw you last night, what were you doing in Branksome? I was waving at you but you just stared straight at me, as though you hadn't seen me.'

I told her, 'I was at home getting the evening meal for the children and my husband.' Then I asked her what I had on. 'The same as you did at work this morning,' she replied. But the strange thing was, she said I just stared straight ahead, not seeming to see anything or anyone. My duplicate was seen standing by a wall. The place was on the main road, where she had to stop her car. The area is quite open so you can easily see someone. I told her that it was impossible it was me, but she was certain it was.

Brenda Collins says that her double has been seen on two previous occasions, the first time in 1956, when she was a schoolgirl, and the second time in 1963, when she worked as a hairdresser. On the latter occasion she only learned of her duplication when a customer bitterly complained that she had been ignored by her in Woolworths. 'I saw you and spoke to you, but you didn't even seem to know I was there,' she fumed. 'How could I speak to you if I wasn't there?' retorted Brenda, who was at work when the incident occurred. But her denials did not convince the customer, who was so upset by Brenda's perceived rudeness that she never returned to the shop.

It is of course upsetting when you are seemingly ignored in that manner, and I well remember being upbraided by an acquaintance about a quarter of a century ago, for apparently passing him in the street on three or four occasions without speaking to him or even acknowledging his presence. I apologized and vainly protested that I simply had missed seeing him, although he was adamant that I had looked right at him. I still have no idea if I was actually there, or if unbeknownst to me my double was out taking a stroll. Yet if it was my second self, then I'm glad it doesn't ramble about very often on its own, because it's just an embarrassment when it does!

The double that the Reverend Sabine Baring-Gould (1834–1924) once passed also failed to answer him when he spoke to it, yet it was seemingly aware of his presence. This perhaps suggests that it was only partly conscious. Baring-Gould's description of the encounter appears in *A Book of Folk-Lore*:

The Waking Double

Some years ago I was walking through the cloister at Hurstpierpoint College, when I saw coming towards me the bursar. I spoke to him. He turned and looked at me, but passed without a word. I went on to the matron's apartment, and there the identical man was. I exclaimed: 'Hallo, P., I have just passed you and spoken to you in the cloister!' He turned very pale and said, 'I have not left this room.' 'Well,' said I, 'I could swear to an alibi any day.'

However, readers of *Supernatural Disappearances* will remember the strange visit that the double of my Aunt Peggy's partner Nigel made to her late one summer afternoon, when he was actually in the process of driving home from work. Nigel was fully awake (or at least I hope he was!) at the time, whereas Peggy had just roused herself from an afternoon nap when she saw him apparently come into the room. Hence her experience perhaps reflects the heightened awareness to sub-threshold stimuli that waking people seem to enjoy; it is also an example of how the likeness of someone who is being waited for – especially if he has been delayed – can travel ahead of him to alert those concerned of his approach.

Peggy and Nigel live in Hastings in East Sussex, and at that date, which was either 1985 or 1986, Nigel was working in Eastbourne. He always left work shortly after 5 p.m., and in the summer time, owing to the greater number of cars on the road and the resulting traffic jams, he usually arrived home at around six o'clock, sometimes later.

On the day in question Peggy had done her usual afternoon chores, which included preparing their evening meal and laying the table, and then had sat in an armchair by the lounge window, where she dozed off.

I woke to hear Nigel's voice calling out – 'I'm home, dear' – and saw him crossing the room towards me. He came over to my chair, and bent and kissed me, saying,

'Oh, that journey. Won't I be glad when I retire.' . . . I jumped up quite flustered. 'Goodness, I didn't know it was that late. You go and get changed. I'll put the oven on and pour you a drink.' I attended to these things and called, 'Your drink's poured.' After about five minutes and hearing nothing, I looked in the bedroom and bathroom, but he was not to be seen. I thought he had gone back out to the car for something. I went outside but there was no car in the drive or garage. Then, for no explainable reason, I looked at the clock. The time said 5.40, at least 20 minutes before he could possibly arrive. He was not at home. He eventually arrived home at 6.15.

Peggy said that Nigel's double was seemingly solid and lifelike in appearance and that she definitely felt its kiss on her cheek. She rose from her chair as it turned from her, so that she saw its rear view as it left the room. But what is particularly significant is that neither of the couple's two small dogs, who always waited by the front door for Nigel to return home, made any sound to signify his return nor did they come frolicking into the living room with him, as they always did, which suggests that they were quite unaware of the double, even though it was seen, felt and heard by their mistress.

Although Nigel says he can't remember specifically thinking about Peggy when his duplicate turned up in their living room, we can easily appreciate how the frustration he felt stemmed from his wish to be out of the crawling traffic and at his destination, which was back at home. This may therefore have been the trigger that prompted the projection of his double once he was under way again, and so led to a partial fulfillment of his wish.

Similarly, a Mr G.A.K.'s double, as reported in *Light* magazine, once entered his dining room, in which a woman friend was sitting, when he was in fact upstairs, and its actions were very similar to those of Nigel's double:

[My double] opened the door of the dining room and entered. Walking over to the lady, this semblance of myself gazed earnestly at her for a moment or two, and then departed, leaving the door open, from which she distinctly felt a draught . . . I should mention that the light was subdued, but sufficient to show that the face of this apparition seemed paler than natural. I was engaged in conversation at the time, and the phenomenon was without apparent cause or meaning.

I once managed to consciously leave my body in my double form, within which I felt entirely solid and normal, and Tibetan and other Eastern adepts can bring about such separation at will for practical ends. For most of us such intentional projection is difficult to bring about, and when managed, usually only happens once in a lifetime. The following cases are further examples of how a wish or desire to be where the body is not became a reality.

Sometime before the last war (he doesn't, unfortunately, give the exact date) Elliott O'Donnell, the well-known writer on ghosts and hauntings, was walking from Nancledra back to his home in St Ives, Cornwall, a distance of about three and a half miles, 'when the idea of projecting myself came over me,' he says, 'and I began to concentrate very earnestly on being in my house'. He had made numerous previous attempts to bring such a projection about, but without managing to do so.

I was quite alone, there was not a soul in sight, and everywhere around me was very still. After a while I was able to visualize my house, at first rather hazily, but finally with a clearness that was most remarkable and startling.

The vision was brief. It abruptly faded away, and I was back again on the white, dusty road. When eventually I arrived at the house my wife greeted me with: 'How naughty of you to frighten us so. Where did you vanish to?'

Asked to explain, she told me that about an hour previously she and everyone else in the house had heard me enter the house, cross the hall, and call out to her. On running into the hall to greet me, she had found no one there. Nor was there a sign of me anywhere.

This case has much in common with Nigel's projection into Peggy's bungalow, for although Elliott O'Donnell's double wasn't seen by those in the house, its footsteps and the other noises it made on entry were heard, as was the sound of its voice calling out a welcome. Mrs O'Donnell also felt the same sense of astonishment and unease as Peggy had when her search of the house revealed that her husband wasn't there.

Indeed, Elliott O'Donnell's brief awareness of the interior of his house, which he saw with startling clarity, reminds me of the experience that Canadian folklorist Helen Creighton had in 1954, when she was lecturing at Indiana University. One day she received some worrying news about her ailing elder sister, who had apparently been taken seriously ill in Nova Scotia. It put Dr Creighton in a terrible quandary, as she didn't know whether she should return home or not. She wrote:

> [My sister] was constantly on my mind until one day while I was walking across the campus I was for a fleeting moment in the house where she was living, and I had a picture of life proceeding normally. Someone walked quietly through a room and no one was disturbed in any way. I knew then that the trouble had righted itself, and subsequent letters showed this to be true.

If this was a projection of Helen Creighton's double, then it is another example of how the second self can be sent elsewhere and thus used in a practical way to help the 'real' person, who cannot be where the double goes.

Zelma Bramley-Moore describes how one evening, when she was sitting in her drawing-room, accompanied by a female friend, and reading a letter, her double was seen by a maid in her bedroom upstairs. The two women heard the maid apparently speak to Mrs Bramley-Moore, ask her what she was doing in the dark, click the light switch on for her, and then scream. Moments later she came rushing down the stairs in a state of terror. On seeing Mrs Bramley-Moore there 'she stared and stared' at her, but gradually recovered herself enough to explain what had happened.

> Madam, as I passed your bedroom door it was wide open, and there was no light in your room, but I could see you quite distinctly standing just inside the door; you were looking at yourself in the mirror, and you had your arms up and were arranging your hair. You were wearing your white satin dress [that evening I was dressed in black]. I spoke to you, and switched on the light, when you immediately vanished.

There is no obvious reason why Zelma Bramley-Moore's double appeared in her bedroom, where it was seen by the maid, and she herself provides no clue to this in her account of the event. It is possible, however, that while she was reading the letter she may have wondered about the state of her hair and perhaps wished that she had worn her white dress in preference to the black one. Such idle but intense thoughts might have projected her double into her bedroom, quite unknown to herself, where it in effect carried out her wishes.

Yet it is less easy to account for the anomalies in the following case, which was collected by Helen Creighton in her native Nova Scotia. One evening, she says, Mrs Sadie Clergy of East Petpeswick went to a summer dance with her husband. Also at the dance was Mrs Young, a stout, auburn-haired lady who that night was wearing a black dress (like the real Zelma Bramley-Moore). The two women were friends and they later talked together until the time came for Mr and Mrs Clergy to leave, although Mrs Young decided to stay at the dance for a while longer. The couple began walking home, but when they arrived at a bend in the road they suddenly heard Mrs Young's voice behind them calling out, 'Sadie, why don't you wait for me?' They turned, but while Mr Clergy was unable to see anyone there, his wife clearly saw her friend, although looking quite different from when she had left her. The woman's hair was now completely white and she had a white silver shawl thrown around her shoulders. Mrs Clergy gaped at her in astonishment, but before she could say anything the figure of Mrs Young disappeared from view. When Sadie asked Mrs Young the next day what had become of her, her friend said that she had not left the dance for a long time afterwards and that what she (Mrs Clergy) had seen was not her.

The figure on the road was evidently the double of Mrs Young, which oddly had acquired the characteristic paleness of doubles by wearing a replicate white silver shawl (which the real woman did not have with her) and by whitening its hair. Doubles, it seems, do not like wearing black! And although it was perfectly visible and apparently solid and real to Sadie Clergy, the latter's husband could not see it at all, which again suggests that some psychic ability on the part of the observer is necessary (at least on occasion) for a double to be viewed. Mrs Young had no idea that her double had been projected, yet it may be that, once the Clergys had left the dance, she wished she had walked home with them, which desire was sufficient to send her double after them.

The next case, which happened in the United States, is one of the most remarkable on record, involving as it does the witnessed and distant appearance of the double of a man who was himself confined in a mental asylum.

On 14 June 1854, one Alexander Ferguson, having some two months earlier become noticeably more unstable, unpredictable, and violent, was readmitted to the Indiana Hospital for the Insane at Indianapolis, the state capital. He was then about 46 years old and unmarried, and his life as a farmer had filled out his large frame, making him a formidable opponent to anyone who upset him or got in his way, while his countenance, noted Dr E.V. Spencer, one of the three physicians who examined him, 'is not wild but (he is) a shrewd cunning fellow by looks'. At that time he lived in New Harmony, Posey County, in the far south-west corner of Indiana, some 150 miles from the capital.

Alexander Ferguson was in fact no stranger to the inside of mental institutions. He had been confined in the Lunatic Asylum at Lexington, Kentucky, his birth state, during the period 1838–39, from where he had escaped after six months, albeit 'much improved both mentally and morally'. His improvement, however, seemingly owed more to the episodic nature of his illness and to his enforced abstinence from alcohol, than to the treatment he received, for the obsolete remedies there employed, which included putting him in a large barrel and pouring cold water on his head, were as useless as they were barbaric.

Yet fortunately, the care of the mentally sick in Indiana had been revolutionized in 1848 by the building of a new Insane Hospital, situated on the outskirts of Indianapolis (see Figure Three), whose first Superintendent, Dr James S. Athon, introduced the most up-to-date and effective methods of treatment then available, and a humane regime. Indeed, one of his early, albeit temporary, successes was Alexander Ferguson, who was first admitted to the Insane Hospital as patient number 68 in August 1849, and although he refused to take any medication, maintaining that he was perfectly sane and did not require any, he was released as 'recovered' on 6 May 1850.

Figure 3   Indiana Hospital for the Insane

Alexander's mental state, following the ten-year hiatus since his incarceration in Kentucky, had been unbalanced, noted Dr Mark Trafton, by the 'intemperate use of alcoholic drinks to which may perhaps be added the occasional severe blows which he received on his cranium in the rows which he very frequently became involved from his reckless course'. Yet oddly, Dr Trafton later on in his report contradicts this violent portrait by claiming that '(Alexander) has never attempted to injure himself or anyone else although he sometimes threatens to fight those whom he supposes to be his enemies'.

Alexander's second admission to the Indiana Hospital for the Insane came at the request of his guardian, H.C. Cooper of New Harmony, following his attempts to injure his brother, Ashberry Ferguson, and other members of his family, and, indeed, 'any one around him'. But once back inside, Alexander remained as obdurate as ever against taking medication, and became daily more home-sick for his friends and for the familiar haunts of New Harmony.

But then, in mid March 1855, according to medical author Dr S.B. Brittan, the Superintendent of the Insane Hospital, much to his surprise, had an unexpected visit from two Posey County members of the Indiana Legislature. They told him that they had received angry letters from several of their constituents, who complained that on 27 February Alexander Ferguson had been seen 'wandering at large in neighbourhoods near his old home; that the citizens were afraid of him, and were anxious that he should be returned to the institution without delay.' And they demanded to know how such a thing could possibly have happened.

The astonished Dr Athon told the legislators that either they were the victims of a practical joke or else those in Posey County were sorely mistaken as to the miscreant's identity, because inmate Alexander Ferguson had not been released at any time. With this assurance, which was confirmed by members of Dr Athon's staff, the pair went away shaking their heads, wondering which of the two alternatives was true.

But if James Athon thought he had solved the problem, he

received another shock the next day when a letter came from Alexander's guardian H.C. Cooper. It likewise claimed that Alexander had been seen in the locality, and the writer insisted on knowing when he had been released and why. Dr Athon replied in a similarly confident manner, although this time he emphasized that a mistake had most probably been made by the so-called witnesses. He reaffirmed that Alexander Ferguson was still a patient at the Insane Hospital and that he had not been allowed out since the day of his arrival.

Dr Athon's letter brought a speedy reply from Mr Cooper, who gave a detailed account of the different places where Alexander had been seen and what he had done, and revealing that 'his movements were closely observed by several persons who had been familiar with him for years. The witnesses concurred in saying that he did not look well, that he was pale, and that he was indisposed to converse; but not one entertained the slightest doubt of his identity'.

This testimony prompted the puzzled Dr Athon to interview Alexander, whose answers to his questions unfortunately puzzled him even more. For on asking Alexander when he was last in New Harmony, the lunatic smiled mischievously and replied that he had made a flying visit there three weeks before. The bemused Dr Athon gently pointed out to him that that was impossible, as he hadn't been let out of the Hospital since his arrival there on 14 June 1854. Alexander, however, insisted that he spoke the truth:

I tell you that I did go. My spirit flew down there quick, and left this pair of clothes, and the rest of me that you see here in the ward to take care of the Antichrist, and keep the Devil out of the bathroom.

He went on to describe where he had been, whom he had met, and what he had said and done, which included a visit to a local distillery, where he had drunk a quantity of whisky, all of which, Dr Athon was amazed to note, agreed with the depiction of his purported movements and actions reported

by both Alexander's guardian and by the Posey County legislators. And if that wasn't enough, the lunatic spoke colour-
fully of his return through the air to the Insane Hospital:

> I didn't see anybody on the road – I was so high up; came
> with the pigeons; they was a-cheering me – ha! ha! ha! –
> and didn't make no time at all; I got home first; I'm going
> back tomorrow. The whisky ... made my head swim –
> run against the lightning, which singed my whiskers –
> coloured 'em red. The truth is, Doc, they are all crazy.

This is, as I mentioned earlier, one of the most remarkable
and persuasive double cases on record, for it seldom occurs
that a person is under lock and key when his or her double is
seen by numerous witnesses at a distant site. It is also remarkable for the fact that Alexander's double flew through the air
to Posey County and back again, whereas the double is usually projected straight to such a faraway place. And because
Alexander's consciousness left his awake self with his double,
he was not only fully aware of the journey in both directions
by air but also of all that he did and said when he arrived in
Posey County. Yet in other respects, such as his double's paleness and its actual disinclination to talk, it is similar to the
other cases I have examined.

And although we can see a reason for Alexander's out-of-
body experience in his strong wish to be at home again, it is
less easy to understand why it should be so singular, unless his
insanity somehow made it easier for his double to vacate his
body along with his consciousness. If so, then this accords
with the general notion that mental upset and anxiety tend to
promote double separation.

However, the Venerable Mary of Agreda was also aware of
travelling through the air (in her double form) to and from
the New World, and of converting, while there, the heathen
Jumano Indians to Christianity. The double of this celebrated
seventeenth-century Franciscan nun appeared numerous
times on the other side of the Atlantic Ocean in New Mexico,

while she herself, having fallen into an ecstatic trance, remained in her cell in Spain.

> In her voyages to New Mexico [writes Michael Geddes, an early biographer], she had seen prodigious seas and vast tracts of land, all of which she gave a perfect account: she had been in some of them by day and in others by night; in some of them she had met with fair weather, and in others with rain; and had seen the Indians on their knees to her praying for a remedy.

I have fully considered Mary's amazing bilocatory missionary journeys in my previous book entitled *Supernatural Disappearances*.

Three other sightings of doubles in the nineteenth century are worth recording here, not least because they involved famous people, namely the poets Lord Byron and Percy Bysshe Shelley, and the author Mark Twain.

In July 1809 George Gordon, Lord Byron (1788–1824), left England for a grand tour, the *de rigueur* European excursion for young aristocrats, which took him to Spain, Malta, Greece, the Aegean Islands, and Turkey, and which lasted for almost two years. It was the making of him, both as a man and a poet, and his experiences while away formed the basis for his first poetic masterpiece, *Childe Harold*.

Towards the end of 1811, a few months after his return to London, he ran into an old school friend, Sir Robert Peel, who was then Secretary for Ireland and who of course later became famous, when Home Secretary, for the organisation of the London police force. And Sir Robert, whose name still distinguishes the London bobby from his country cousins, startled Byron by insisting that he had seen him in the capital when he was abroad. As Byron wrote to John Murray:

> He told me that in 1810 he met me as he thought in St James's Street, but we passed without speaking. He mentioned this – and it was denied as impossible – I being then in Turkey.

But if Lord Byron was able to dismiss that incident as a clear case of mistaken identity, he was surprised to discover that he was seen a second time by his friend, who was then in the company of his brother.

A day or two after he pointed out to his brother a person on the opposite side of the way – 'there' – said he 'is the man I took for Byron' – his brother instantly answered 'why it is Byron & no one else'.

But that wasn't the last time Byron's double was apparently seen in London, for Peel told him that not long afterwards he had been spotted:

... by somebody to *write down my name* amongst the Enquirers after the King's health – then attacked by insanity; Now – at this very period, as nearly as I could make out – I was ill of a *strong fever* at Patras, caught in the marshes near Olympia – from the *Malaria*. (Byron's italics)

We may reasonably suppose that Byron's illness was the cause of his double projection on this third occasion, for negative factors such as stress, mental confusion, and sickness can all prompt such separation. And while we don't know what brought about the first two double incidents, it's possible that he suffered a bout of home-sickness while away that was sufficiently intense to send his double back to London. There is an intimation of this in one of the early verses of *Childe Harold*, which describes the outwardly stoical hero sailing away from his native shore:

> And fast the white rocks faded from his view,
> And soon were lost in circumambient foam;
> And then, it may be, of his wish to roam
> Repented he, but in his bosom slept
> The silent thought, nor from his lips did come
> One word of wail, whilst others sate and wept,
> And to the reckless gales unmanly moaning kept.

While Byron was obviously surprised by what Peel told him, he was sufficiently impressed by the accounts, and by his friend's manner, to be persuaded that he was neither mistaken nor misguided, although the poet recognized the incongruity of such duplication. He wrote:

> I do not disbelieve that we may be *two* by some uncommon process – to a certain sign – but which of the two I happen at present to be – I leave you to decide. – I only hope that *t'other me* behaves like a Gemman (i.e. a gentleman).

Yet whereas Byron's double turned up in distant London, that of his friend and fellow poet Percy Bysshe Shelley made its appearance in and around his foreign holiday home, where it too was seen on three different occasions.

In April 1822, Shelley and his wife Mary, the celebrated authoress of the gothic novel *Frankenstein*, who had been staying at Pisa, in north-west Italy, rented a house called the Casa Magni, which stood right on the rocky shoreline of the Gulf of Spezzia, near the small town of Lerici. They moved in with another married couple, Edward and Jane Williams, who were old friends of theirs.

Figure 4   Percy Shelley's double seemingly presaged his death by drowning

The Casa Magni had a terrace, which ran along its whole frontage, below which there was a sheer drop into the sea. The windows of the large central dining room and of the two front bedrooms, that stood one on each side of it, looked out on to the terrace and the sea beyond. One June day, while on the terrace, Shelley met his own double, which said to him 'How long do you mean to be content?' and then vanished, which not surprisingly frightened and upset him, although Mary Shelley comments in her description of the event (in a letter to Maria Gisborne) that 'Shelley had often seen these figures when ill', despite the fact that it was she who was sick at the time. Shelley himself was then in perfect health, if somewhat overtired. (The poet also saw himself a second time, which appearance is considered in the next chapter).

Not long afterwards the double of Shelley was also seen on the terrace by Jane Williams, which necessarily heightened the message of impending doom implied by its first appearance. Mrs Williams was looking out through one of the dining room windows on the day in question, along with a visiting friend, the writer Edward Trelawny (1792–1881), when:

. . . she saw as she thought Shelley pass by the window [writes Mary Shelley], as he often was then, without a coat or jacket – he passed again – now as he passed both times the same way – and as from the side towards which he went each time there was no way back except past the window again (except over a wall twenty feet from the ground) she was struck at seeing him pass twice thus & looked out & seeing him no more she cried – 'Good God can Shelley have leapt from the wall? Where can he be gone?' 'Shelley?' said Trelawny – 'no Shelley has past [*sic*] –'

The poet himself was absent from the house, and some way off from it, at the time, which further reveals that it was his double that Jane Williams saw and not the actual man. This is likewise suggested by the curious fact that while she was able to see the double, which passed by twice in front of her, Edward Trelawny (like Mr Clergy), who stood next to her, could not. The invisibility of the double to one or more of those present is difficult to account for, unless its sighting does require a certain psychic sensitivity, which Trelawny and Clergy presumably lacked.

The dénouement of these grim appearances is surely familiar to most. On Monday, 1 July 1822, Shelley and Edward Williams sailed from Lerici to Leghorn aboard the poet's undecked yacht *Ariel*, in order to visit Leigh Hunt. Then, in the early afternoon of 8 July, they left Leghorn to return to Lerici, a voyage that should have taken them about seven or eight hours. But a bad storm broke out shortly afterwards, and they never reached port. Ten days later their drowned, badly abraded and decomposing bodies were found on the shore between Pisa and Spezzia. Both were later cremated, on following days, on that same shore, attended by many mourners, among whom were Lord Byron and Leigh Hunt.

It is thus strangely and beautifully ironic and revealing that Shelley includes in one of his greatest poems, *Adonais: An Elegy on the Death of John Keats*, the lines:

> *Peace, peace! he is not dead, he doth not sleep –*
> *He hath awakened from the dream of life –*
> *'Tis we, who, lost in stormy visions, keep*
> *With phantoms an unprofitable strife,*
> *And in mad trance strike with our spirit's knife*
> *Invulnerable nothings –*

Or that he ends it with the following incredible prophecy:

> *. . . my spirit's bark is driven,*
> *Far from the shore, far from the trembling throng*
> *Whose sails were never to the tempest given;*
> *The massy earth and sphered skies are riven!*
> *I am borne darkly, fearfully, afar;*

Whilst, burning through the inmost veil of Heaven,
The soul of Adonais, like a star,
Beacons from the abode where the Eternal are.

Mark Twain is the pseudonym of the American author and humorist Samuel Langhorne Clemens (1835–1910), who is famous around the world for books such as *Tom Sawyer* and *Huckleberry Finn*. He had a variety of jobs before he began writing, which included time spent as a Mississippi riverboat pilot (from where he picked up his pen name 'Mark Twain' being the cry uttered by the man taking depths readings, meaning two fathoms), while later, in 1861, he mined for silver near Carson City, Nevada.

It was in Carson City that he became good friends with, among others, a young Canadian woman, a Mrs R. They later lost contact with one another, and it was more than twenty years before they were destined to meet again, during which busy and creative period, when many of Twain's books were published, she passed right out of his mind. Their reunion happened in the mid-1880s, when Twain and fellow author George Washington Cable (1844–1925) went on a publicity tour together, which took them to Montreal, where they were given a reception at the famous Windsor Hotel, whose capacious interior and echoing corridors I remember well from my time spent there.

> It began at two in the afternoon in a long drawing-room in the Windsor Hotel [writes Twain]. Mr Cable and I stood at one end of this room, and the ladies and gentlemen entered it at the other end, crossed it at that end, then came up the long left-hand side, shook hands with us, said a word or two, and passed on, in the usual way.

Then to Mark Twain's absolute surprise and pleasure he suddenly noticed Mrs R. among the press of people entering at the far end of the room.

I knew her instantly; and I saw her so clearly that I was able to note some of the particulars of her dress, and did note them, and they remained in my mind. I was impatient for her to come. In the midst of the hand-shakings I snatched glimpses of her and noted her progress with the slow-moving file across the end of the room, then I saw her start up the side, and this gave me a full front view of her face. I saw her last when she was within twenty-five feet of me. For an hour I kept thinking she must still be in the room somewhere and would come at last, but I was disappointed.

Mark Twain had, of course, no idea what had happened to Mrs R., except to suppose that for some pressing reason, such as another engagement, she had been obliged to slip out of the room before she reached him. He did not see her leave, but his attention had been constantly distracted by the hand-shaking and brief chats with the other people in the queue. Hence while Twain was intensely disappointed at missing meeting Mrs R. again, he had no reason to suspect that anything out of the ordinary had occurred.

This assumption was to change that evening, when he went to a nearby lecture hall to give a talk. Soon after he arrived there, someone told him that a friend of his was in the waiting room, who wished very much to see him. Twain immediately guessed that it was Mrs R., and he hurried off to speak with her, not wanting to miss her again.

There were perhaps ten ladies present, all seated [he recalled]. In the midst of them, was Mrs R., as I had expected. She was dressed exactly as she was when I had seen her in the afternoon. I went forward and shook hands with her and called her by name and said:

'I knew you the moment you appeared at the reception this afternoon.'

She looked surprised, and said: 'But I was not at the

reception. I have just arrived from Quebec, and have not been in town an hour.'

Thus while Mrs R. was seen at the afternoon reception by Mark Twain, the real woman was not there. She was in fact many miles away at the time. The author had therefore clearly and unmistakably seen her double, which remained in the queue and had continually changed its position, along with the others as they snaked their way around the edge of the room, for probably more than one hour.

This case strongly attests the external nature and physical reality of the double. For if Mark Twain had mentally generated the figure of Mrs R. he would have pictured her as he remembered her twenty years earlier, not as she then was and certainly not in the clothes that she would wear later that evening. Moreover, if we alternatively argue that Mrs R.'s thoughts and expectations of meeting Twain telepathically caused him to create an image of her likeness, it would none the less have been impossible for him to have found a person-sized slot in the queue for it to fit into, especially one that maintained the same space, within the moving queue, between itself and those ahead and behind. This suggests that the double was actually there, and that, in addition to it being visible to Mark Twain, it was a physical reality to those lining up to meet him.

Yet we may suppose, however, that it was those same excited thoughts and expectations that prompted the double of Mrs R. to come ahead of her, and to thereby announce her later arrival to her old friend, which indeed it successfully did.

Two recent double cases that have been kindly sent to me further reveal the strange variety of this fascinating phenomenon. Both coincidentally share a hospital setting, although the second concerns a man who was unconscious at the time his double was seen.

The first happened a little over ten years ago to the aforementioned author Dennis Bardens and took place at the Royal Masonic Hospital in Hammersmith, while he was convalescing after a period in intensive care. He writes:

I was sitting alone on a first-floor balcony looking down on to the front entrance and the garden, when the main door swung open and a tall, grey-haired man in a patient's red dressing gown came out and walked slowly and deliberately into the sunlit garden. I was astonished to see him followed by the exact duplicate of himself, solid and clearly delineated in the bright sunshine.

The double remained in view for several minutes and a few feet behind the man; it also kept in step with him and otherwise imitated his movements. Such mimicking by doubles happens quite often. The strange and unexpected sight had Mr Bardens wondering if it was caused by the drugs he was taking, and he looked around to see if there was a nurse or anyone else whom he might call to verify what he was seeing. But unfortunately there was no one, although he was able to satisfy himself that the figure was being independently trailed by its double and was not therefore an illusion.

I continued to watch intently, having established by moving my eyes around that absolutely nothing else was double. I was too ill at that time to bother to mention it to anyone and it must remain a mystery.

The second case happened in the summer of 1994 at the Frenchay Hospital, Bristol, and was reported by nurse Sian Roberts. On the day in question, one of her patients, a man whom she identifies as Alan, underwent a major spinal operation which began at 9 a.m. and lasted until two o'clock in the afternoon. It was during this lengthy operation, when Alan was unconscious and incapable of movement, that his double appeared to two fellow patients whom he had met only the day before in the patients' day room. They were then in their hospital ward and both were waiting to have an operation later that day, about which they were understandably more than a little anxious – although they had not, says Nurse Roberts, expressed their fears to Alan. However, it was to assuage their apprehension in this regard that Alan's double made its appearance to them. Nurse Roberts writes:

> Alan appeared to them at 11 a.m. and looked solid and real. He also reassured them both that there was nothing to worry about and that they would both make full recoveries. When Alan appeared he was wearing his theatre gown . . . The two gentlemen on the ward had not received any drugs nor did they have a history of hallucinations or dementia, etc. The double of my patient was not cited by anyone else and a case of mistaken identity has been eliminated. Alan only became aware of the incident a week later (medical staff had not told him) when all three men met in the patients' day room and the two men thanked Alan for the kindness he showed them on the day of their operations!

The appearance of Alan's double while the man himself was unconscious is not at all surprising because a lack of consciousness is, as we have seen, conducive to such separation. We must take notice that his double could speak and that it was dressed in a replica of his hospital gown, which was entirely right for the occasion. Indeed, both of the men it appeared to thought it was the real person until they learned later that he was anaesthetized at the time. What is remarkable, however, is his double's knowledge of the outcome of their operations, which appears to have been genuine prescience and not a conventionally spoken 'Oh, don't worry, you'll be all right', such as any one of us might say in such a situation. But whether this knowledge belonged to the double or was brought by it from Alan, is an open question. If the former, we must ask if this means the double can only gain such knowledge when it is free of its physical envelope; if the latter, we must ask if the presence of the double within the physical body somehow impedes the conscious awareness of foresight, and if it does, why should it?

5   Seeing Oneself

A figure in the terrible distance moved towards me
As relentlessly as day advances upon night,
Nearer it came and slower I
Went out to meet it.

It was myself.

From *Encounter* by Leonard Clark

To see one's own double is perhaps the most frightening phenomenon of all, not least because it often, although by no
means always, forebodes one's own death.

And while we can perhaps explain the appearance of a seriously ill person's double to himself as the result of a loosening of whatever internal bonds hold the double in place during health, it is far less easy to understand why someone sees
himself if he subsequently dies in, say, an accident. The latter
implies foresight – but does the double possess it, or is the
double merely the way by which the foresight of the person
is expressed to himself?

Yet seeing oneself may also be an entirely neutral event,
without any future consequences – while on rare occasions
the double may actually save the life of the person whose likeness it bears, which not only gives it a positive meaning but
also indicates that it is aware of the danger lying ahead.

And remarkably, a person's double may not always be
immediately recognizable to him, possibly because it isn't
reversed like a mirror-image and thereby lacks the positional

113

body clues with which we are most familiar. Such was the experience of Sheila of Hereford, whom we met in an earlier chapter.

> I also think I met myself. That was in Devon. I'm a hospital almoner and we were having a garden fete, when suddenly I met somebody and I said, 'Oh, how lovely to see you' – and we rushed at each other, and then, a second thought came: 'Oh, but I don't know you' – and we both turned away to the right. I looked for the person later but I never saw her again. I was wearing a grey costume and she was dressed in a very similar fashion to myself. It was rather peculiar.

Needless to say, if Sheila did come face to face with herself, then her double's presence held no grim significance for her, as she is still alive and well.

However, there are many cases on record where the opposite is true. Queen Elizabeth I, for example, saw herself shortly before her death, and as if to symbolize her royal rank, her double was distinguished by its unusual appearance.

The event is described in a manuscript entitled *The relation of the Lady Southwell of the late Q(ueen's) death*, written in April 1607, which reads:

> She fell downright ill, and the cause being wondered at by my Lady Scroope, with whom she was very private and confidential, being her near kinswoman, her Majesty told her (commanding her to conceal the same), 'that she saw one night her own body exceedingly lean and fearful in a light of fire'. This vision was at Whitehall, a little before she departed for Richmond, and was testified by another lady, of whom the Queen demanded 'Whether she was not wont to see sights in the night?' telling her of the bright flame she had seen.

114

The incident took place, as Lady Southwell says, at Whitehall, which dates it to the beginning of March 1603. The emaciated appearance of Elizabeth's double seemingly reflected how she would look, and was thus, in this regard, ahead of its time. Although Lady Scroope makes no mention of the Queen being frightened by the sight of her own self, her reluctance to take to her bed when she began to feel sick perhaps indicates that she was aware of its significance. Her double's appearance in 'a light of fire' is also unusual; this may have been the result of a brightening of the inner light that some (if not all) doubles possess.

Later in the same century two daughters of Henry Rich, the first Earl of Holland (1590–1649), who successfully pressed the suit of Prince Charles (later King Charles I) for the hand of the French princess Henrietta Maria, saw themselves not long before they died. John Aubrey records that it was the unmarried and beautiful Lady Diana Rich, who:

> as she was walking in her father's garden at Kensington, to take the fresh air before dinner, about eleven o'clock, being then very well, met with her own apparition, habit, and every thing, as in a looking-glass. About a month after, she died of the small-pox.

However, Aubrey's comment that the figure appeared 'as in a looking-glass' means only that it exactly resembled Diana Rich on that particular morning, clothes and all, and not that it was a reversed image, such as she would actually see in a mirror. Furthermore, because the incubation period of small-pox is less than one month, it would seem that Lady Rich became infected with the virus some time after she saw her own double; hence in this regard it was certainly prophetic.

The other daughter of Henry Rich who saw herself was Isabella, the wife of Sir James Thynne, who was not only beautiful, like her sister Diana, but also an accomplished lutenist. Yet Aubrey says no more of the incident than that she 'saw the like of herself also, before she died', while elsewhere condemning her with the observation, made originally by Tacitus about Agrippina, that 'All qualities she had, save a pure mind'. However, Isabella Thynne's beauty and musical talent (if not her smuttiness) inspired the poet Edmund Waller (who was once, coincidentally, the MP for Hastings) to write several poems about her, although only one is identifiable from its title, the lovely *Of My Lady Isabella, Playing on the Lute*, which I will quote in full to give the reader a more intimate awareness of her:

> *Such moving sounds from such a careless touch!*
> *So unconcerned herself, and me so much!*
> *What art is this, that with so little pains*
> *Transports us thus, and o'er our spirits reigns?*
> *The trembling strings about her fingers crowd,*
> *And tell their joy for every kiss aloud.*
> *Small force there needs to make them tremble so;*
> *Touched by that hand, who would not tremble too?*
> *Here love takes stand, and while she charms the ear,*
> *Empties his quiver on the listening deer.*
> *Music so softens and disarms the mind,*
> *That not an arrow does resistance find.*
> *Thus the fair tyrant celebrates the prize,*
> *And acts herself the triumph of her eyes:*
> *So Nero once, with harp in hand surveyed*
> *His flaming Rome, and as it burned he played.*

Let me also mention in passing that my school was at Hadham Hall in Hertfordshire, the former seat of Arthur, Lord Capel, who was beheaded along with Henry Rich and fellow Royalist the Duke of Hamilton on 9 March 1649. Hence I can't help but feel a certain affinity with those two daughters of Henry Rich, who saw themselves.

Another monarch who had the dubious pleasure of encountering her own double was Catherine the Great. Born Princess Catherine of Anhalt-Zerbst, at Stettin in Germany, on 2 May 1729, she married the dim-witted and physically feeble Peter Feodorovich, a nephew of the Empress Elizabeth of Russia, in 1745. When Elizabeth died in 1762, the cretinous Peter succeeded her, but not long afterwards Catherine, with the help of Cossack Gregor Orloff, the first of her thirteen lovers, had him strangled, and thereby became empress herself. Catherine was to rule single-handedly for another thirty-four years, during which time she considerably enlarged Russia's empire and thereby earned, like Alexander of Macedon before her, the title of 'the Great'.

Catherine encountered her double in the throne room of her Moscow palace, which she unsuspectingly entered one day along with Comte de Ribaupierre and a number of other high-ranking officers and ladies, although the exact date of the incident is uncertain. She evidently was the first to notice the ersatz version of herself, for she suddenly pointed, to everyone's surprise, at the imperial throne, where her likeness had had the temerity to seat itself. What happened next is astonishing, to say the least:

> After a moment of dead silence the great Catherine raised her voice and ordered her guard to advance and fire on the apparition [narrates Lady Napier]. The order was obeyed, a mirror beside the throne was shattered, the vision had disappeared, and the Empress, with no sign of emotion, took the chair from which her semblance had passed away.

This was an incredibly rash act, for the double can in fact be injured like the real person, while the damage it sustains simultaneously afflicts him or her. Hence Catherine could have been harmed, possibly fatally, by ordering her double to be shot at. This possibility can of course only be countenanced if the double is an external, three-dimensional entity in its own right, which was seemingly confirmed by Catherine's double being sighted by everyone accompanying her into the throne room. However, because there is no mention of the imperial throne sustaining any shot-damage, while the mirror beside it was broken by the firing, we may perhaps conclude that the guard aimed their muskets to one side of the Empress's double and not directly at it.

Two other eighteenth-century examples of such self-seeing are sufficiently different from the average to warrant their inclusion here. The first relates to a man who was saved from death by his double, and the second, by contrast, tells how another was beaten up by his!

In the year 1749, the Bavarian composer Christoph Gluck (1714–84) paid a brief visit to Ghent, in Belgium, where he stayed in lodgings. One night, having dined with friends, he returned home on foot and was surprised to notice a man walking ahead of him in the moonlight, who not only exactly resembled him in height, dress and manner, but who took the same route through the narrow streets as he did, which gave the composer the eerie impression that he was following himself! Gluck's surprise turned to astonishment when his double – for so the figure appeared to be – marched up to the door of his lodgings, opened the door with a key it took from its greatcoat pocket, and went into the building. Scared by what he had seen and not daring to follow his double inside, Gluck hurried back to the house of his friends, to whom he blurted out what had occurred and begged them to allow him to spend the night there. His friends, though surprised, immediately agreed, if only to calm the trembling composer.

The following morning Christoph Gluck, accompanied by those same friends, returned to his lodging. All were curious to find out what, if anything, had happened and what thereby the double had signified. When they climbed the stairs to Gluck's room, they were shocked to discover that it had been cordoned off. Pushing open the door, they first noticed the dust that lay thickly everywhere, then the gaping hole in the ceiling where a heavy, dark-coloured roof beam had fallen from it to drop squarely on to Gluck's bed. If the composer had been asleep there he would certainly have been killed. But fortunately, the timely appearance of his double prevented that from happening, and had thereby saved Gluck's life.

Gluck, of course, like most people who are awake, had no idea that his double had left his body, and indeed he was able to carry on perfectly well without it. More significantly, the double was able to preserve his life because (in addition to knowing what might happen) it found in its duplicate pocket a duplicate door key with sufficient substance to open the lock, while the figure itself had enough mass and strength to rotate the said key and to push open the door. This not only means that the double was really external to the composer, but was endowed with at least some of the properties of ordinary matter.

That being so, it is perhaps easier to accept the following strange account of a double that Martin Martin, a native of the island of Skye, included in his *A Description of the Western Isles of Scotland*, published in 1703, a copy of which accompanied Dr Samuel Johnson and James Boswell on their famous journey to those remote parts seventy years later.

According to Martin a man living near Barvas, on the island of Lewis, was troubled by the repeated nearby appearance of his own double, although it was quite invisible to anyone else. When he was outdoors it would irritate him exceedingly by asking 'many impertinent questions', although it kept silent when he was indoors. Finally the self-tormented man told a neighbour what was bothering him, and he, after some deep thought, advised him to throw a burning coal at the double's face.

> The man did so the next night, and all the Family saw the action; but the following day the same Spirit appear'd to him in the Fields, and beat him severely, so as to oblige him to keep to his Bed for the space of fourteen days after. Mr Morison Minister of the Parish, and several of his Friends came to see the man, and joined in Prayer that he might be freed from this trouble, but he was still haunted by that Spirit a year after I left Lewis.

Had I not previously shown that the double is a genuine, quasi-physical phenomenon, it would be easy to dismiss this story as nothing more than an account of how someone saw repeated hallucinations of himself. Such an hypothesis is indeed seemingly supported by the fact that no one else saw the figure, although I have already explained that the double is often only visible to those who are somehow sensitized to its presence. And furthermore, if the man had thrown a live coal at an hallucinatory figure, why would he afterwards beat himself up so badly that he'd need a fortnight in bed to recover from his injuries? It does not make sense. Indeed, the man's injuries seem more likely to have resulted from the attack of an angry double, than to be caused by his own fists.

This is by no means an isolated case, although it is unusual for someone to be set upon by his own double. In this respect, it is worth mentioning here the attack made upon a nineteenth century stage-coach driver by the double of his sweetheart, as he was driving his equipage through woods on the shore of Loch Awe, in county Argyll, Scotland. To his astonishment the real girl, as he thought, suddenly appeared beside him, grabbed the whip from his hand, and beat him so badly with it that he was obliged to turn the coach around and return home. When he had recovered, the man sought out the young woman and angrily upbraided her for the attack. However, she insisted that it was not her, for as her family would attest, she had been at home all night, although she had been, she admitted, very worried for him at the time. This was because she had learned that the inhabitants of a house at which he was due to stop had gone down with the plague, and she feared he might contract the fatal disease from them. Hence it seems that her acute anxiety for her lover's safety projected her double on to his stage-coach, albeit without her knowing, and so allowed it to take the violent measure it did in order to save him from a worse fate. This surely means that her double was unable to speak to him, which thereby forced it to act so desperately.

Another man who met himself was the poet Wolfgang Goethe (1749–1832), the author of *Faust*. This is how Germany's most famous literary son described the incident:

I was riding on the footpath towards Drusenheim, and there one of the strangest presentiments occurred to me. I saw myself coming to meet myself on the same road on horseback, but in clothes such as I had never worn. They were light grey mixed with gold. As soon as I had aroused myself from the day-dream the vision disappeared. Strange, however, it is that eight years later I found myself on the identical spot, intending to visit Frederika once more, and in the same clothes which I had seen in my vision, and which I now wore, not from choice, but by accident.

The double of himself that Goethe saw was not simply dressed in different clothes, like Zelma Bramley-Moore's double, which wore a white dress while the real woman downstairs wore black, but was rather clad in a costume that he would not wear for another eight years. This may mean that the image he saw did not derive from himself as he then was, but was instead himself as he would be, which if so means that he was somehow able to see through the divide that separates 'now' from 'then' and descry himself riding along the same track in eight years time. Hence it was a sort of time-shift. It is of course a pity that Goethe does not describe the horse his replica was riding, for if it was 'the future' horse, it would make that possibility more certain.

And interestingly, in his youth Heinrich Heine (1797–1856), Germany's second most famous poet, wrote a poem entitled *Der Doppelgänger*, which soon afterwards (in 1826 or 1827) the composer Franz Schubert set to music, along with five other Heine poems, to form a song cycle called *Schwanengesang* (Swan-song). The double has always played an important part in German folklore and tradition, and many sightings of doubles have been recorded (and publicized) in Germany right down to the present day. This is why the German term *doppelgänger* has been adopted into the English language and why it often takes precedence over English alternatives.

Doubles

I have put Heine's poem *Der Doppelgänger*, which casts
the narrator's double as a romantic expression of his own
past hurt feelings, into the following rhyming English version, like the original:

> *The night is still, and empty the thoroughfares;*
> *In this old house once lived my dearest dear.*
> *When she went away I was broken down with cares,*
> *But her darling house it is still standing here.*
>
> *There also stands a man, gazing up wretchedly,*
> *Wringing his hands like one whose heart has died.*
> *I start and tremble when his tearful face I see;*
> *The moon reveals it is myself those tears have cried.*
>
> *You pitiful double, pale lonely semblance,*
> *Why do you mimic the grief of yesterday*
> *That tore in two my heart? Unkind remembrance*
> *Of all those dismal nights, after she went away.*

We have discussed how in June 1822, the poet Percy
Bysshe Shelley saw his own double on the terrace of the Casa
Magni, a house in Italy at which he and his wife were staying
with Edward and Jane Williams. The incident is made even
more interesting by its apparent foreboding of Shelley's death
and by the fact that his double spoke, saying 'How long do
you mean to be content?' Such a verbal address by one's own
double is very unusual, for the simple reason that we would
not expect it to be conscious. Yet by speaking, Shelley's double showed itself to be not entirely devoid of mental ability.

Shelley saw himself again a few days later, an event that
occurred one night after he had woken from a nightmare in
which he was confronted by the lacerated and evidently
drowned figures of Edward and Jane Williams, of whom
Edward spoke, saying to him, 'Get up, Shelley, the sea is
flooding the house and it is all coming down'. The shock of
this pronouncement woke Shelley and caused him to spring

out of bed and rush to the window, through which he seemingly saw waves about to crash into the house. Yet as he stepped back the scene changed and, to his horror, he was suddenly confronted by a double of himself trying to strangle his wife Mary, who was in actuality asleep in the bedroom on the other side of the dining hall. This so alarmed Shelley that he ran across to her room, although he avoided immediately rousing Mary for fear of frightening her. She was, however, startled into wakefulness by the noise he made and jumped up, which fortunately caused the terrifying vision that Shelley still saw of his double throttling her likeness to vanish.

It's possible of course that Shelley may have dreamed both scenarios. Yet while the sighting of waves about to crash into the house was probably a postscript to the dream about Edward and Jane Williams, the heightened perceptions the poet would have experienced as he came into full consciousness allowed him to then see his double trying to strangle that of his wife. Yet why was it doing such a terrible thing?

To answer this we may suppose that if Mary's double had left her sleeping form and walked into Shelley's bedroom, it may have gone unrecognized by Shelley's own exteriorized second self, which lacked full consciousness because he was dreaming, and was seen as a threat to his sleeping body – and was therefore attacked by it. But when Mary awoke her double would have been drawn back into her body, which allowed Shelley's, the perceived threat gone, to return to his, and which in turn explains why the dreadful 'vision' disappeared then.

The double is most likely to leave a person's body when he or she is asleep, and this naturally means that more doubles are wandering about during the hours of darkness. But doubles are vulnerable to attack, as we have seen, by other doubles, perhaps maliciously, with the added complication that any harm they suffer reciprocally affects their physical self. Now it's well-known that most deaths happen at night, when people are asleep. Might this be because the sleeping person's double goes walkabout and gets attacked, and the shock of the unexpected assault reciprocally causes the real individual's heart to stop?

In 1823, an overworked and mentally exhausted William Hone (1780–1842), the writer and editor, saw his own double as he walked in London. He rather oddly describes the incident in the third person:

> [He] left home in the afternoon to consult a medical friend, and obtain relief under his extreme depression. In Fleet-street, on the opposite side of the way to where he was walking, he saw a pair of legs devoid of body, which he was persuaded were his own legs, though not at all like them. A few days afterwards when worse in health, he went to the same friend for a similar purpose, and on his way saw himself on precisely the same spot as he had imagined he had seen his legs, but with this difference that the person was entire, and thoroughly a likeness as to feature, form, and dress. The appearance seemed as real as his own existence.

I cannot accept that Hone was right in supposing the 'pair of legs devoid of body' were his duplicate limbs, for as he states, they did not resemble his own. However, such incomplete doubles have been reported by others, although it is usual for the top half to appear rather than the bottom half.

Where the second, complete figure is concerned, which was his double, Hone was of the opinion that 'the illusion was an effect of disordered imagination', rather as Christoph Nicolai had dismissed the figures he had seen, yet it beggars belief to suppose that Hone could (or would) somehow mentally create an exact self-image, which he saw as if it was external to himself. Rather, it is easier to accept that his double was actually walking along the other side of the street. Yet if so, Hone was entirely unaware that it had left his body.

Exactly forty years later, in 1863 at Sibberton in Northamptonshire, the double of a young married woman named Sarah Hall manifested in her dining room when she and her husband and their two guests were together there. The account is taken from *Phantasms of the Living*.

> One night, when we were having supper an apparition stood at the end of the sideboard . . . we all four saw it, my husband having attracted our attention to it, saying, 'It is Sarah,' in a tone of recognition, meaning me. It at once disappeared. None of us felt any fear, it seemed too natural and familiar.

Sarah Hall was as surprised as the others by her double's appearance, and she was unable to suggest any reason for it. She was, it seems, perfectly well at the time. What makes the incident even more unusual is that her double, like Goethe's, was dressed differently from herself, being clad in a 'spotted, light muslin summer dress' whereas she was wearing a warm dress suitable for the chilly autumn season. Indeed, she did not then possess such a dress, although she reportedly 'wore one like it nearly two years afterwards'. Does this mean that Sarah bought a dress similar to the one her double had worn – or did her double select a dress like the one it knew she would wear, which implies it possessed precognition? Or alternatively, did Sarah and her companions see herself as she would be, which means they had a collective view into the future, as Goethe alone appears to have done? But while these questions remain unanswerable, it is fortunate that Sarah's double had no baleful meaning, as both she and the others lived for several years afterwards.

Such was not the case for the French foreign legionnaire who saw himself walking towards himself only moments before he died. His experience was reported by Wellesley Tudor Pole, who was there at the time (1918), although neither he nor those with him saw the man's death-fetch for themselves. Yet the stricken soldier was uplifted by what he saw:

> When seemingly beyond speech, he half rose from the pillow in the sand where he had tried to take refuge

from the sun, and cried out in broken French [I trans-late], 'Why, there is myself coming to meet me. How wonderful!' Then he fell back and died and we reported the incident on reaching Bou Saada the next day.

But while seeing oneself has a particularly grim reputation, the sighting must, so tradition also relates, be interpreted with regard to the time of day. Evening sightings, as we have seen, are reputedly the most ominous, whereas morning ones are usually fortunate in meaning. Elizabeth I's double was seen before her death both by herself and, on another occasion, by her lady-in-waiting during the evening, while Lady Diana Rich, who also died soon afterwards, saw hers at eleven o'clock in the morning. Christoph Gluck and Sarah Hall, however, both saw their own doubles in the evening and survived the experience, contrary to traditional expectations, although it's possible that Gluck walked home after midnight and so saw his double in the early hours of the following day. Goethe saw his double in the morning and, true to form, not only lived for many years afterwards but grew in fame, and William Hone came to no harm after seeing his double in the afternoon. The Scottish peasant survived his double's beating, which was perhaps an effective compromise as he had seen it on both numerous mornings and evenings, while the day-time sighting of his double spelt doom for the hapless French legionnaire.

Security supervisor Adrian Brown is another person who saw his own double during the evening and thankfully survived the experience. The surprising and frightening encounter took place at 11.15 p.m. on a cold night in February 1991, when the twenty-six-year-old was on patrol in his van and heading towards a gravel extraction pit close by Wareham, in Dorset, which formed part of his nightly round. What makes the incident so unusual is that Mr Brown didn't see himself standing at the side of the road or walking across it, but instead was passed by himself going the other way in a double of his own van!

After stopping at one of the several small roundabouts on the road, Adrian Brown was surprised to see a van exactly like his own come around it from the opposite direction and then drive by him. He said:

As the van passed, three or four yards from me, I saw – clearly illuminated by the street lamps and headlights – myself. It was me. It was like looking in a mirror. I looked for five or six seconds as the van passed. The other 'me' glanced across – the sort of cursory look you make as you pass another vehicle. There was no hint of recognition. I was amazed. Then perplexed. It took me a few minutes to digest what had happened. I carried on driving. Then I felt very frightened. I had goose bumps and the hair on the back of my neck stood on end. The strangest and most horrific thing was that it was not someone who looked like me. It was *me* – a carbon copy.

Furthermore, Adrian Brown's identification of himself is based upon more than the visual sighting. For apart from being the only driver from his firm booked out on mobile patrol that night, none of the other drivers resembled him in the least, and, perhaps most convincing of all, the company's other van was off the road for repairs. He's also adamant that his sighting of himself wasn't a mistaken impression caused by tiredness.

I know it wasn't the product of an over-active imagination. While I was doing shift-work I was always on the ball. The nature of the job demanded that I kept alert and wide-awake. I was not tired and had only just begun my shift which went on until early next morning.

Adrian Brown regrets that he didn't take the opportunity to follow himself, but admits it was his fright that stopped him. It took him a few days to recover from that; and the experience certainly wasn't something he'd wish to repeat.

Yet the oddest aspect of his encounter with himself was the associated duplication of his vehicle, which his double was driving. But can we really believe that such a large, complex multi-part machine using both petrol and electricity was replicated along with himself? If so, how did it happen? And what about Mr Brown's clothes, and those manufactured items like hats, keys, and spectacles we have met with in other cases? Were they really duplicated in a similar way? This intriguing possibility is examined in the next chapter.

With the exception of Shelley's double, which said a few words, the doubles of these people were all mute, and seemingly lacked the power of speech. Indeed, this is typical of such self-image doubles. It is seemingly explained by the consciousness of the person concerned not transferring itself to the double, which results in it lacking awareness and cognition.

But this cannot be the whole story. For while a self-image double may be dumb, some at least have an awareness of their surroundings and the associated ability to control what they are doing, which enables them to perform certain tasks. After all, the double of Christoph Gluck successfully found its own way through the streets to the real man's lodgings, whose door it unlocked and through which it went, while the double of Adrian Brown had no difficulty driving the duplicate van in which it was seen.

This indicates that the double probably carries with it a part at least of the person's consciousness, which is sufficient to allow it to behave as it does and which is not missed, so to speak, by him or her. Such a division of consciousness, unlikely though it sounds, is evident in the account given by Sir Auckland Geddes, the eminent professor of anatomy, of his near-death experience, which happened during a period of illness. He remarks:

I realized I was very ill . . . thereafter at no time did my consciousness appear to be in any way dimmed, but I suddenly realized that my consciousness was also separating from another consciousness which was also me. These, for purposes of description, we could call A and B consciousnesses, and throughout what follows (my awareness was attached) to the A consciousness . . . the A consciousness, which was now me, seemed to be altogether outside my body, which it could see. Gradually I realized that I could see, not only my body and the bed on which I was lying, but everything in the whole house and garden . . .

This may be a paradigm for what happens when the double spontaneously originates from someone who is awake, except that the person's awareness remains within himself, that is, in what Geddes calls 'consciousness B', while 'consciousness A' departs with the double yet does not produce any awareness of itself within him. However, if the double's consciousness leaves memory traces, the real person may become aware of these later on. They may surface, for example, in his dreams or they may eventually result in a *déjà vu* experience.

Yet despite the double's quasi-physical nature and its ability to behave just like the real person, it is essentially a temporary phenomenon. No double has ever been able, at least as far as I can determine, to remain apart from the real person and thus take up a separate existence of its own. Something, it seems, always draws it back to its real self, and the time it can spend apart from him or her probably has a maximum length of five or six hours, although most separations are much shorter. The probable reason for this is that the double, like the body, has certain energy requirements, which are not only likely to be high but which it cannot replace on its own once its stored energy is used up.

This may explain why the double often vanishes from sight like a ghost. For without energy it becomes unable to maintain its form, with the result that it visually fades away while at the same time being drawn back into its physical source.

6   Doubles of Non-living Objects

Yet arms like England's did he wield,
Alike the leopards in his shield,
Alike his Syrian courser's frame,
The rider's length of limb the same . . .
        From *Marmion* by Sir Walter Scott

I have previously mentioned the doubles of non-living objects, notably the clothes that are worn by the doubles of people. The very idea of duplicated garments often prompts laughter in the sceptical, who find it ludicrous to suppose that doubles (or ghosts, for that matter) should appear dressed, even if such a thing were possible, and believe it implies the images are imaginary and merely reflect the propriety of the witnesses.

Yet it is entirely reasonable to expect doubles to be clothed. After all, we ordinarily dress ourselves, and few would even wish to wander around naked. Hence a double without clothes is a contradiction in terms, as it would not be a replica of the real person. And even where the unaware or zombie-like double is concerned, if there is some prior involvement of the person's consciousness in its separation, as there surely must be, then this will automatically insist that its likeness is clothed, much as a parent dresses a child before letting it out of the house.

The thrust of the sceptic's criticism, however, has less to do with the desire of the double, or of the real person, for it to

131

be clad than with the seeming impossibility of clothes and other non-living objects being duplicated. Yet the sceptics have presumably forgotten that most clothes, for instance, are made from natural materials, like cotton, wool, leather and silk, which were once alive and whose fibres may still therefore retain their original duplicate 'essence'.

However, it was the ancient Egyptians who maintained that everything in nature, whether animal, vegetable or mineral, has a ka or double, which comprises a sort of energy field within and around them, and which will, when separated from its physical source, replicate its form. Thus not only do we humans have a double, but so also do other living things, as well as objects that were never alive, including those which are manufactured, like clothes, weapons, pottery, furniture, and even buildings. These also have a surrounding aura that can likewise be seen, as I know from my own observation.

The double of someone who is awake generally presents itself in replicas of the same clothes that he is wearing at the time, although as we have noted they are sometimes different. And likewise, the double may be seen carrying duplicates of whatever the person is holding in his hands. Here are two accounts of such double sightings that were featured in the pages of *Light* magazine. Mrs A. Penny wrote:

> My husband's duplicate appeared once in a most point-less and unexplainable way. He was seen from a window of his house coming up the drive, *with exactly the same dress*, gait, looks, and pace of movement with which he was wont to approach it several days in every week, when returning from Exeter, four miles off; only, it was more than an hour before the usual time . . .

While Mr G.A.K. describes how, on another occasion, his double was seen by his wife:

> Coming home one evening, she saw me walking hurriedly from a tramcar, carrying a small paper parcel, and

apparently entering the house before she came up. She was, of course, surprised to find that I was not really there, but I arrived about half an hour later, exactly as I had appeared, and with *the same kind of packet in my hand.*

Both cases involve the doubles of men that arrived home not long in advance of the real individuals, just as the double of Nigel, my Aunt Peggy's partner, walked into their living room about thirty-five minutes before he really came home. His double, too, was dressed in exactly the same clothes that he was wearing at the time.

A very interesting double appearance is mentioned in *Phantasms of the Living*, which describes how, during the sickness from typhoid fever of Helen Alexander, a lady's maid, at a country house at Torpoint, Cornwall, she was visited by the double of her mother, which rather surprisingly brought with it a replica candlestick. A servant named Frances Reddell was attending Helen Alexander at the time, who said:

I heard the call-bell ring . . . and was attracted by the door of the room opening, and by seeing a person entering the room whom I instantly felt had to be the mother of the sick woman. She had *a brass candlestick in her hand, a red shawl over her shoulders, and a flannel petticoat on which had a hole in the front.* I looked at her as much as to say, 'I am glad you have come,' but the woman looked at me sternly, as much as to say, 'Why wasn't I sent for before?' I gave the medicine to Helen Alexander, and then turned round to speak to the vision, but no one was there. She had gone. She was a short, dark person, and very stout.

Not long afterwards Helen Alexander died and two days later her parents and a sister arrived to take charge of her body. Of her meeting with the deceased's mother, Frances

Reddell says 'it gave me a great turn when I saw the living likeness of the vision I had seen two nights before'. She told the sister about the incident, who commented that 'the description of the dress exactly answered to her mother's and that they had brass candlesticks at home exactly like the one described'.

We can only wonder why Mrs Alexander's double brought a duplicate of one of the real woman's candlesticks with it, unless Mrs Alexander was holding one at the moment her double vacated her body, but that it did is certainly suggestive of the reality of object doubles. We must also take special note of the ringing of the call-bell and the opening of the door, which both reveal that Mrs Alexander's double was able to manipulate ordinary matter much as the real person could, and that instead of the sick woman's double visiting her, which is what usually happens in a near-death situation, the reverse occurred. An accompanying letter of verification mentions that Helen Alexander had written to her sister when she first became ill, but had made light of her condition, and adds that no other message was sent either by the sick woman or by anyone else prior to her death. Hence no one at her home, which was in Scotland, knew that she was terminally ill, although it later transpired that on the final evening her mother had gone up to bed remarking, 'I am sure Helen is very ill'. This intuitive feeling and the anxiety it must have aroused presumably prompted the visit by her double, although Mrs Alexander herself was apparently quite unaware that 'she' had been in her sick daughter's bedroom.

It is not known what Mrs Alexander was actually wearing when her double appeared in her dying daughter's bedroom. No questions were put to her about this as it was thought best in the circumstances to say nothing of the incident. Hence if she was still dressed in her day-clothes, she may or may not have been wearing the red shawl and the flannel petticoat, or alternatively, she may have been, as seems most likely, clad in her night attire. However, that she possessed and often wore a red shawl and a flannel petticoat with a hole in the front was confirmed by her other daughter.

Another case from the same volume records how John Rouse, a resident of Croydon, met the double of a lady named Mrs W. one moonlit night while he was taking a walk on the outskirts of Norwich, where he had gone on business. Mr Rouse and Mrs W. knew one another well, for both were interested in spiritualism and had attended many seances together. Indeed, at the time of the incident Mrs. W. was taking part in a seance at Croydon. John Rouse writes of the meeting:

I could plainly see that the figure before me was a *well-dressed lady in evening dress*, without bonnet or shawl. I could see *some ornament or flower in her hair, gold bracelets on her bare arms, rings on her fingers, and could hear the rustle of her dress* . . . in the next minute I felt certain that I had seen the lady before, and immediately afterwards I recognized her as Mrs W. I had not the least fear, for she was so real that I thought she had, like myself, unexpectedly and suddenly got to Norwich . . . We approached within about 5 feet of each other; she gazed at me very intently as I thought; she held out her hand to me, and I could see her face and lips move as if about to speak to me. I was in the act of taking her hand to greet her, but had not touched her, when some iron hurdles which formed the fencing of the cattle market rang as if they were being struck with an iron bar. This startled me, and unconsciously I turned round to see what made the noise. I could see nothing, and instantly turned again to Mrs W. but she was gone.

It later turned out that Mrs W. had fallen into a trance at that time (about 11 p.m.), which had alarmed her fellow sitters, who experienced some difficulty in bringing her out of it. And when she was later asked to comment on John Rouse's account of what had happened to him, Mrs W. wrote:

I quite remember the seances and the particular occasion to which Mr Rouse refers, when I became unconscious one night, at about 11 o'clock, and on recovery had no recollection of anything but that *I had gone suddenly out of myself. My dress at the time of the occurrence is stated quite correctly* . . . I have never had the same experience before nor since then.

But although we might expect the double of a person to be clad in replicas of what he or she is wearing at the time, this is by no means always the case. Yet as a general rule, the clothing of the double of someone who is awake is typically the same, whereas that worn by the double of someone who is asleep is often (although not always) different. The reason for this seems to lie in what the person regards as appropriate clothing for the scene or company into which his double is projected, and this naturally suggests that his consciousness is involved in making such a decision, even when he is asleep.

Thus we can understand why the sick and sleeping Mrs Goffe's double felt able to appear in a nightgown in her child's bedroom, in which the only other adult was a female nurse; why the double of the sleeping Caroline H. appeared one night in the bedroom of another female servant clad in her nightgown and with her hair hanging down; and indeed, why my double put an ersatz dressing gown on over its pyjamas to look around the door of my mother's bedroom one morning – although such examples do not help explain why the double of the sleeping Sheila of Hereford appeared fully dressed in her mother's bedroom, unless of course she had been, in her dreams, planning to go somewhere else afterwards.

A similar and perhaps more understandable difference between the dress of the double and that of the sleeping person was witnessed in the seventeenth century by a Mr Trahern, the son of a shoemaker in Hereford, who described his experience to John Aubrey:

One night as he lay in bed, the moon shining very bright, he saw the phantom of one of the apprentices, sitting in a chair *in his red waistcoat, and head-band about his head, and strap upon his knee*; which apprentice was really in bed and asleep with another fellow-apprentice, in the same chamber, and saw him. The fellow was living, 1671.

The double of the apprentice was evidently dressed in replicas of the real boy's working clothes and with other accoutrements of his trade, which he would normally wear or be possessed of when out of bed. However, it may well be that the apprentice boy was dreaming of being at his work, in which case he would have pictured himself as described, whereupon his double, on leaving his body, put this into effect.

A recent case, which was collected by Joan Forman, nicely illustrates the decorum of the sleeping mind or of the double, so that the latter appears appropriately dressed for the situation in which it finds itself. In the mid-1970s, at 10.15 on a Saturday morning in Hereford, a woman named Mrs Pauline Parker had the pleasure of meeting up with, or so she thought, an old friend of hers, a Captain Daintry (not his real name) of Llanidloes, in Montgomeryshire, where she had once lived.

He took my arm, said 'Lovely to see you, girl, after all this time', and we were about to enter into a lengthy chat when I remembered he had been very ill, he is old (about 78) and it was very cold and noisy in the street, so I told him I was meeting my husband for coffee in the Green Dragon, in about twenty minutes and invited him to join us. He said he would love to meet Derek again, and was going to the Green Dragon anyway, and so we parted.

But Captain Daintry did not turn up at the appointed time, and eventually the Parkers had to leave the Green Dragon without seeing him. However, Mrs Parker dropped him a note of apology, and by way of compensation, invited the elderly man to visit them the next time he came to Hereford.

The couple were therefore understandably surprised when Captain Daintry wrote back to say that, while he had some 'vague recollection' of meeting Mrs Parker somewhere, he certainly had not been in Hereford the previous Saturday. Thinking that he was getting forgetful, Mrs Parker, in an effort to jog his memory, wrote back and described exactly where they had met, the time of their meeting, what was said, and *'what he had been wearing'*.

> In reply, he told me that he had given a dinner party on the Friday evening and on that Saturday morning he had felt unusually tired and had asked his housekeeper to give him breakfast in bed, which she did, and he came down about 10.45 a.m. The housekeeper corroborates this.

The real Captain Daintry had therefore not been in Hereford on that cold Saturday morning, although his double, dressed appropriately for the occasion and the weather, had been. Moreover, the double not only had sufficient substance to appear exactly like the real man at close quarters, but it was able to take hold of Mrs Parker's arm with enough strength for its grip to be felt, and it was also able to speak to her, which implies that it had both breath and a larynx to enable it to form words, as well as sufficient intellect to know what it was saying.

A late-nineteenth century case records how Mary Murnane of Philadelphia, in the United States, saw the double of her aunt walk towards her in the street, two days before she died in Limerick, Ireland. Mrs Murnane was naturally astounded to see what she at first thought was the real woman, and assumed she must have miraculously recovered from her illness (consumption) and had somehow crossed the Atlantic to reach Philadelphia:

This opinion was quickly changed as we approached each other, for our eyes met, and she had the colour of one who had risen from the grave. I seemed to feel my hair stand on end, for just as we were about to pass each other she turned her face towards me, and I gasped, 'My God, she is dead, and is going to speak to me!' but no word was spoken as she passed on ... *She held a sun-shade over her head, and the clothes, hat, etc., were those I knew so well before I left Ireland.*

Here again we find that the double of a bed-ridden woman not only chose to dress itself (or was dressed by the woman's consciousness) in a replicated version of a costume suitable for a city street, but selected one that was instantly familiar to her niece. The double also carried, oddly enough, a duplicated sunshade, which in reality it could hardly have needed.

Finally, where clothing is concerned, Catherine Crowe records the mysterious sighting of the double of a German woman named Madame Dillenius one night in her own bedroom, where the real woman was in bed, attired in her nightgown, with her six-year-old son, who, on seeing his replicate mother, awoke both her and her sister-in-law, sleeping in the other bed. The frightened sister-in-law screamed at Madame Dillenius: 'I see you double! you are in bed, and yet you are walking about the room.'

The face of Madame Dillenius's double had a very sad expression and was leaning its head upon one of its arms; it was also, even more strangely, wearing a copy of the black dress Madame Dillenius had bought herself shortly before. Her son, disliking the sight of this unhappy, sombrely-clad visitor, apparently sprang out of bed and tried to push 'her' out of the room, crying, 'Go away, you black woman', but without any success. Not long afterwards it disappeared. The terrified Madame Dillenius naturally thought that the figure foreboded her own death, but this did not happen, although her husband was involved soon afterwards in a serious accident. Hence the appearance may have been in anticipation of this event, which points to prescience on the part of Madame Dillenius.

We may suppose that when the double appears in facsimiles of the real person's clothes, jewellery and other ornaments that he is wearing at the time, it acquires them from the original items when it leaves his body. Thus the clothes and so on contain their doubles within and around themselves, which are already enclosing the double of the person, and they all become separated and projected together from their physical counterparts. The same will presumably apply to any object the person is holding.

However, it is less easy to understand what happens when the double presents itself in facsimiles of clothes and jewellery that are different from those the person is wearing. It seems hard to believe that the naked, newly emerged double goes to the person's wardrobe and selects facsimiles of a particular set of wearing apparel from the clothes' rack or the shelves, and then slips into them like the real person would. Can Zelma Bramley-Moore's double really have said to itself, 'Well, she's wearing black, but I much prefer myself in white'? Probably not, but it may mean that the real Zelma had thought she might look better in white, and this concern with her appearance prompted her double to leave her body and not only to examine itself so clad in her mirror but also to arrange its hair at the same time. If so, then the person's thoughts must play the principal role in this process, and we may therefore surmise that their concentrative power somehow causes the doubles of the clothes and ornaments in question to be projected from their location within those items to around his own double.

Such a hypothesis makes it easier to understand how Adrian Brown saw himself driving a facsimile of his own van. After all, at the time of the incident Adrian Brown was driving in his van to a gravel extraction pit at Wareham, in Dorset. It was night, his security job was not the most exciting of occupations, and the lengthy trip out to the Wareham pit was tedious. We can therefore imagine how Adrian Brown may well have wished that he had already completed the call and was driving back to Bournemouth, where he lived. If his desire in this regard prompted his double to do just that, it would naturally have projected along with itself a double of the van in which the real man was driving, for that was the only way it could 'drive back' to Bournemouth.

Such wish-fulfilment may have brought about the appearance of another car in Bexhill, Sussex, not so many years ago. On the day in question Brian S. told his wife Anne-Marie that he had to make a business trip to Horsham, some forty miles away from their home. One hour later Anne-Marie was driving through Bexhill and passed, to her astonishment, her husband driving in the opposite direction. When Brian came home later that day, she said to him, 'I thought you were going to Horsham,' to which he replied, 'I did'. 'You couldn't have,' she retorted, 'because I saw you in Bexhill.' As might be expected, this led to a heated argument between the pair, which 'nearly caused us,' adds Brian ruefully, 'to divorce'. But Brian swears he was not in Bexhill that day and had gone to Horsham, while his wife is equally adamant that she did see him driving through Bexhill. Hence if Brian is not lying and if his wife did see him, then she must have spotted doubles of him and his car. And if so, these could both have been generated or projected in the same way that Adrian Brown and his van probably were, that is, by Brian's wish to be home translating itself into its partial realization through his double and that of his car.

From earlier times there are a number of reports of how the doubles of horse-drawn carriages, with replica people aboard, have been seen. Typically, these pass by a short time before the real conveyance and its occupants, which leads me to suspect that they may have been mentally projected in a similar way to the above-mentioned cars, although it is admittedly harder to accept that people other than the driver, and the horses, are so produced. Of particular interest in this regard is the 'double sighting' reported by Andrew Lang, which happened when he was staying at a Highland castle.

One day a fellow guest, a woman, said to her nephew, 'So you and Susan did drive in the dogcart; I saw you pass my window.' To which the nephew replied, 'No, we didn't; but we spoke of doing it.' This suggests that her nephew's and Susan's like-minded thoughts somehow resulted in their doubles uniting briefly with those of the dogcart and its horses, which enabled them to go for a brief (and observed) excursion together.

Andrew Lang mentions another case which has all the hallmarks of a double sighting, in that the carriage and its occupants were not only seen out of doors in a country spot, but through a gap in a hedge, yet disappeared when the witness tried to make contact with them.

One afternoon towards the close of the nineteenth century, a Mr Hyndford took a ride in the New Forest, when he suddenly came across a clearing he had not noticed before:

> At this moment, on the other side of some bushes a carriage drove along, and then came into clear view where there was a gap in the bushes. Mr Hyndford saw it perfectly distinctly; it was a slightly antiquated family carriage, the sides were in that imitation of wicker work on green panel which was once so common. The coachman was a respectable family servant, he drove two horses: two old ladies were in the carriage, one of them wore a hat, the other a bonnet. They passed, and then Mr Hyndford, going through the gap in the bushes, rode after them to ask his way. There was no carriage in sight, the avenue ended in a cul-de-sac of tangled brake, and there were no traces of wheels on the grass.

The horse-drawn carriage and its driver and female passengers seemed entirely real to Mr Hyndford, and while the carriage was 'slightly antiquated' there was nothing so obviously ancient about either it or the clothes of those aboard to suggest that they belonged to a former time. After all, a Morris Minor car might nowadays be termed 'slightly antiquated', but there are still plenty of them about. And yet the carriage, horses and people mysteriously vanished like ghosts – or like doubles or wraiths, for that matter. So which were they? Unfortunately we can't answer that question, simply because Mr Hyndford did not recognize any of the people he saw and thus he had no idea if they were alive or dead. If the former, then they and the horse-drawn carriage were doubles; if the latter, then they were either wraiths or ghosts.

The question becomes even more vexed when a vehicle without a driver or any passengers is seen. On several occasions in the mid-1930s, for example, an entirely real-looking double-decker bus drove at speed around the corner of Cambridge Gardens and St Mark's Road, near Ladbroke Grove underground station, in Notting Hill, London, obliging on-coming traffic to swerve out of the way, forcing some vehicles off the road, and causing accidents, one of which was fatal, before vanishing without trace. One witness said that 'the lights of the top and bottom deck, and the headlights, were full on but I could see no sign of crew or passengers'. The spectral double-decker stopped appearing for some years after the local council improved the safety of the dangerous corner, which had been the scene of several previous fatal collisions, although Peter Underwood of the Ghost Club Society tells me that it was seen again on a number of occasions in the 1970s and 1980s.

The replica bus seen in the 1930s was of the same type as those then in service, yet unfortunately no one managed to note its registration number in the short period it was visible. Hence we do not know if it was the double of a bus whose route perhaps included the corner where it was seen, or if it was the double of one that had been taken out of service and perhaps sent to the scrap yard. But whether the bus seen in the 1970s and the 1980s should be called a double (or wraith) or a ghost is a moot point. If the real bus still exists, either entire or in parts, then it is a double, but if it does not, as seems likely, then it is a wraith or, alternatively, a ghost. So does 'death' only come to a machine – in the sense that it loses its double form – when its parts are melted down and turned into something else?

One of the most interesting sightings of the double of a non-living object is given by William Hone, although mistakenly under the title of 'Ghost of an Arm Chair' (in *The Every-Day Book*). The married, middle-aged lady to whom the experience happened, had one day kindly ordered that 'an armed chair' which stood in her bedroom should be conveyed to the house of a sick friend, who might thereby have the use of it during her illness. And when evening came the sender went to bed satisfied that she had at least done one good deed that day.

Waking, however, in the night, and looking by the light of the night-lamp at the furniture in her room, she cast her eyes on the place where the said chair used to stand, and saw it, as she thought, in its place. She at first expressed herself to her husband as being vexed that the chair had not been sent; but, as he protested that it was actually gone, she got out of bed to convince herself, and distinctly saw the chair, even on a nearer approach to it. What now became very remarkable was, that the spotted chair-cover which was over it, assumed an unusual clearness, and the pattern assumed the appearance of being studded with stars. She got close to it, and putting her hand out to touch it, found her fingers go through the spectrum unresisted. Astonished, she now viewed it as an illusion, and presently saw it vanish, by becoming fainter till it disappeared.

The rationalist explanation for this curious phenomenon was given by Dr Forster, the medical editor of the *Perennial Calendar*, in which the account first appeared, who explained it by saying that as the woman 'had anticipated seeing the chair in its place, from its always being associated with the rest of the furniture . . . this anticipation was the basis of a corresponding image of spectral illusion'. This is also known as 'expectancy'. Yet the lady had not anticipated seeing the chair in its usual place, for she knew very well that she had ordered it to be sent away. If she expected anything, she expected it not to be there, and to say otherwise implies that she had forgotten what she had done, but there is no evidence for this. And besides, even if she had created a seemingly external image of the chair in her mind as she lay in bed, it seems entirely unlikely that this would remain once she had spoken to her husband, who told her in no uncertain terms that the chair was not there, and certainly not once she got out of bed and walked towards it. Indeed, the chair did not vanish from sight until she tried to touch it.

This suggests that what she saw was not an illusion, but was rather the chair's actual double and thus truly external to herself, standing where the physical chair normally stood. We do not know if the ka or double of the chair was temporarily left behind when the chair was moved, or if it was drawn back later, by whatever forces or energies impinged upon it, or had developed around and within it, during the chair's long stay in the same place. Yet once the double was there, we can be quite certain that by waking in the night, when her psychic vision, if we may call it that, was sharper, the lady was able to see the double and to continue to see it until her increasingly alert mind dulled her psychic perceptions, so causing the chair to fade from sight and eventually vanish. The 'unusual clearness' of the chair-cover and the starry effect of its pattern are consistent with the double being, as I have elsewhere mentioned, a type of energy field.

The above examples seem to show that the doubles of non-living objects are a reality, although quite how they are produced is uncertain. After all, manufactured items like a chair and a carriage consist of several parts, and a bus of very many, which not only have different compositions, but some were once alive, while others were not. Hence is the double of the finished product an amalgam of its parts, like the product itself, or does the finished product somehow generate its own double?

However, we know from Kirlian or high voltage photography, named after its Russian discoverer Semyon Kirlian, that when a piece is cut from, say, a leaf, the corona of light remains in the space left behind and so reproduces the shape of the original leaf, although the removed piece continues to produce a corona, which persists if it is transplanted and lives, but which gradually fades if, and as, it dies. Yet almost exactly the same thing happens, I have noticed, if the corner is torn from, say, a sheet of paper, in that not only does a corona (or double) remain to approximately fill up the space left, but the removed portion immediately acquires a corona around its torn edge. This suggests that although each part of a device or machine brings its own corona with it, once the parts are assembled together they jointly contribute to a merged corona that is unique to the assemblage, namely its double. Hence both of the above alternatives are seemingly true!

There is of course no underlying physical difference between objects that are alive, dead or non-living, as all consist of collections of atoms, which themselves are made of various sub-atomic particles, built up from even smaller units like quarks, which are ultra-minute sparks of energy. And the double, because it has many of the properties of ordinary matter, may well be another energy system that somehow interpenetrates and mimics that of matter. But whether it is derived from the energy of quarks and positrons, etc., or has another, and as yet undiscovered sub-subatomic source – or perhaps one that is purely 'spiritual' – remains for physicists of the future to determine.

7 The Double as Were-animal

'It seems,' I said, looking up at the sun, 'when a man dreams, a white butterfly does be after coming out of his mouth and walking away; and when it comes back again, it is then he awakes.'
From *Twenty Years A-Growing* by Maurice O'Sullivan

As we have seen, there are times when the double of a person, despite its name, is not an exact likeness of its physical source. Such differences usually involve the clothes, the jewellery, or the ornaments it wears, as well as occasionally its hair colour or style, its hirsuteness, its body shape, or even its apparent age. I previously suggested that the former differences reflect the person's will or desire, which prompts the doubles of the clothes and other items of attire he or she would prefer to wear to project themselves at the same time as the double, and to thereby enfold it, or add themselves to it, sometime prior to its manifestation. But while this may be true, it cannot so readily explain those previous differences that might affect the double's actual form.

Even more puzzling are those rare cases when the double takes on a completely different and non-human shape, and becomes, to all intents and purposes, an animal – like a bird, a snake, a wolf or a bear. These ersatz creatures behave like the real animal, although they may also possess the consciousness of the person from whom they derive. Because such doubles have the form of an animal yet originate from a

147

human being, they are distinguished from the real animal, or from even the real animal's double, by having the Old English prefix 'wer' meaning 'man', attached to them, as in 'wer-snake' and 'werwolf,' although an added 'e', as in 'weresnake' and 'werewolf' is now preferred.

The folk belief in werewolves and similar, often nocturnal, were-animals is very ancient and widespread, even today, and cannot be ignored or derided as superstitious nonsense, despite the hostility of scientists. However, there are two variants to the tradition that are quite different, one of which says that a person can physically transform himself into an animal, while the other, by contrast, maintains that it is the double that undergoes the change. And regretfully, our modern writers and film-makers, like yesterday's folk-tale tellers, have preferred the drama of physical shape-changing to that of an animal-double projection, which explains why the first is widely acknowledged, even though it is impossible, while the second is little known, despite it being true.

As we have seen, the Egyptians believed that the khu, or soul, inhabits the heart of a person and is the double of his will and intentions (what we would today call the consciousness), and it was said by them to leave the body at death in the form of a bird and to thereby fly away. This is the oldest representation of the double (or one part of it) in an animal form, although the idea at first sight seems to be nothing more than a primitive way of explaining how the soul is able to escape from the body at death, using a bird (or alternatively a bee, a butterfly, or a scarab beetle) as the familiar image of aerial uplift.

Yet there is far more to the notion than symbolic convenience, as I know from a curious experience that once happened, quite unexpectedly, to me. One night many years ago when I was meditating – or, more correctly, contemplating – in my darkened bedroom, and after having been able to still my mind for some time, I was suddenly surprised to hear, or so it seemed, a small bird fly two or three times around my head. The sound made by its flapping wings was quite distinct

and unmistakeable, and came from no more than a foot
above me. It began without warning, and then, after the bird
had made its circuits, just as quickly ended. On opening my
eyes, which I did not do when the flapping sound was con-
tinuing, I found there was no bird in the room, and neither
was there an open window or door through which a bird
might have flown into, and then out of, it. Hence I can only
assume that the sound was made by some part of my double
making a temporary exit from me in the form of a small bird,
which literally flew around me. The experience was certainly
not hallucinatory, caused by my desires or expectations,
because I did not then know that the double had the ability
to transform itself into a were-animal.

I was particularly reminded of this experience when reading the correspondence of James Howell (1593–1666), published under the title of *Epistolae Ho-Elianae: Familiar
Letters*, as one letter, written on 3 July 1633, contains an
account of the large memorial stone he saw in a stone-cutter's
shop in Fleet Street, London, whose inscription read:

Here lies John Oxenham, a goodly young man, in whose
chamber, as he was struggling with the pangs of death, a
Bird with a white breast was seen fluttering about his
Bed, and so vanished.

Here also lies Mary Oxenham, the sister of the above
John, who died the next day, and the same Apparition
was in the room.

Here lies hard by James Oxenham, the son of the said
John, who died a Child in his Cradel a little after, and
such a Bird was seen fluttering about his head, a little
before he expir'd, which vanished afterwards.

Here lies Elizabeth Oxenham; the Mother of the said
John who died 16 years since, when such a Bird with a
white breast, was seen about her bed before her death.

I was not 'struggling with the pangs of death' when I heard the sound of a bird's wings, although I suppose that contemplation is as close as one can reasonably get to the state of death without actually harming oneself. It is also interesting to note that the 'flapping of death's wings' motif expressing the final moments of a hero's life may not simply be mere literary symbolism after all. Furthermore, my experience and those of the Oxenham family are certainly suggestive of the reported bird-form of the Egyptian khu, although my consciousness was not out of my body when I heard the flapping of its wings.

According to Lady Templeton, the fiancée of Thomas, Lord Lyttleton (1744–79), it was a 'fluttering noise, as of a bird' which preceded the appearance of the ghost of Mrs Amphlett to the 'wicked Lord Lyttleton' on the night of 24 November 1779, at his home in Epsom. Mrs Amphlett had committed suicide following his seduction and abandonment of her. Other contemporaries have described the apparition in somewhat different terms, one saying, for example, that 'a young woman and a robin' appeared together, while another claimed the thirty-five-year-old peer first saw a bird which afterwards changed into a woman wearing white. But whatever the details, most are in agreement that it was either a bird or the sound made by a bird that formed part of the ghostly proceedings.

Yet it wasn't these that frightened the disreputable lord so much as what the apparition said to him, which was that he would die in three days' time at the stroke of midnight. The shaken man did his best to carry on as normal in the immediate aftermath, devoting much of his time to finishing a speech he was due to deliver at the House of Lords on the same day, yet none the less his mood fluctuated between optimism and confidence on the one hand, and gloom and despondency on the other. However, when Lyttleton retired to bed at half past eleven on the third evening, 27 November 1779, he was unaware that Lady Templeton had secretly made sure that every clock and watch (including his own) in the house was half an hour in advance of the real time. By doing this she hoped that, when the false midnight struck and Lord Lyttleton found himself to be still alive, he would weather the real one without harm.

When that midnight sounded, Lord Lyttleton burst out laughing as the last stroke died away, while chiding himself for believing in the foolish prophecy. He summoned a servant and ordered the man to bring him a celebratory glass of wine. Yet when the servant returned with it, he was shocked to discover his master lying unconscious on the floor. On his raising the alarm, Lord Lyttleton's guests ran to the fatal bed-chamber, where they soon determined that he was dead, his pocket watch clutched in his lifeless hand, its time reading half past twelve, the real midnight. So Lord Lyttleton had, despite the best efforts of his fiancée, kept his predicted appointment with destiny.

What makes this remarkable, yet true, case doubly interesting is that at about midnight on that same evening, the wraith of Lord Lyttleton drew back the curtains around the bed of his friend, Mr Andrews (the MP for Dartford in Kent), and told him it was all over. Andrews was so certain that it was the living man playing a practical joke on him, that he threw a slipper at it. The figure retreated into the adjoining dressing room, but when Andrews bounded in there after 'him', he found it to be empty. And a search of the garden outside likewise proved fruitless. It wasn't until the next day that Andrews learned that Lord Lyttleton had died at midnight, and he immediately understood the reason for the wraith's visit, which lay in a light-hearted promise Lord Lyttleton had made to him some years before, to the effect that 'If I die first, and am allowed, I will come and inform you'.

Many early accounts portray the double, when it takes on an animal form, as leaving the body through the mouth, although such an exit is usually reserved, as we might perhaps expect, for those having a small size. Pliny briefly mentions how on one occasion 'the soul of Aristeas was seen to fly out of his mouth, under the form of a raven', which he immediately condemns as 'a most fabulous story', although as we have seen it is not quite as fanciful as he imagined. Aristeas was a well-known Greek poet, the author of *The Tale of the Arimaspians*, and he lived on the island of Proconnesus (now Marmara, in the sea of the same name) during the 6th century BC.

One of the strangest stories of oral egress by a double having the shape of an animal involves Guntram (or Gontram), the Merovingian king of Burgundy, who ruled from AD 561–592. According to the *Historia Langobardorum* of Paulus Diaconus (*c.* 720–790) this monarch went hunting one day and on his return, exhausted by the rigours of the chase, stopped to rest under a tree, where he soon fell into a deep sleep, with his head propped up on the knees of a faithful retainer. Shortly afterwards the retainer was astonished to see a small creature resembling a snake emerge from Guntram's mouth, wriggle down his body and then crawl away across the ground, until a small stream prevented it from going any further. Noticing the snake-creature's evident frustration at this interruption to its progress, the servant drew his sword and laid it across the stream, at which the animal took immediate advantage of the imitation bridge to cross to the other side. From there it made its way to a nearby mountain and, to the man's further amazement, vanished into a hole in the ground.

Several hours then went by before the snake-creature reappeared, and the retainer, who had waited patiently by the hole, followed as it retraced its course back to the king, crawled up his body, and re-entered his mouth. At this, the king woke up and, having stretched himself, told his companion that he had had a marvellous dream, in which he had found himself on the banks of a mighty river, whose rushing waters he had crossed by means of an iron bridge. He next had entered a cavern on the slope of a nearby high mountain, and upon wandering through its inner depths had come to a vast repository of treasure, which had been placed there by

152

his Frankish forefathers. The servant immediately informed the king of what had actually happened, and both were struck by the astonishing way in which the dream had mirrored reality. Guided by this, Guntram ordered the mountain to be excavated at the spot where the snake-creature had disappeared into the ground, and in due course a large and valuable treasure was unearthed, equal to that seen in his dream.

A similar, but socially inverse, story is told by the French chronicler Helinand about one of the retainers of Henry, Archbishop of Rheims, who one day likewise fell into a deep sleep when out of doors. Suddenly, to the astonishment of his companions, a small white-coloured animal resembling a weasel was seen to emerge from the sleeping man's mouth, which then set off, like the snake-creature mentioned above, on a cross-country ramble. The wereweasel was also held up by a stream and a sword was laid over the water to provide a way across for it, although the double did not then disappear down a hole and find a cache of treasure. However, when the man had been rejoined by his wandering double, he awoke and reported that he had dreamed of being in a fine landscape wherein he had crossed a wide river by means of a steel bridge.

I do not know if Helinand's story is merely an updated recapitulation of the first, or if it actually happened, but we cannot fail to notice that the dreams of the sleeping men were really the view of the world (albeit a distorted one) as seen through the eyes of their animal doubles. This suggests, as in the dream cases I have previously discussed, that the doubles carried with them part, if not all, of the consciousness of the sleepers. This is of course a very sophisticated notion, and one that, while wide-spread in the ancient world, is difficult to imagine being formulated by relatively uneducated peoples unless it was based upon actual experience.

Another account of a dreamer who finds himself in the body of his double in an animal form, is told by no less a personage than St Augustine, writing in the eighteenth book of his *The City of God*. The saintly author, perhaps unsurprisingly, blames 'devils' for all such happenings, although he is quite adamant that such dark forces cannot alter the physical shape of a person 'but they can in an indescribable way transport man's phantasm in a bodily shape unto the sense of others . . . while the bodies of the men thus affected lie in another place, being alive, but yet in a trance far more deep than any sleep'. This exactly accords with many examples of the double phenomenon thus far described. He continues:

For one Praestantius told me that his father took [a] drug in cheese at his own house, whereupon he lay in such a sleep that no man could awake him: and after a few days he awoke of himself and told all he had suffered in his dreams in the meanwhile; how he had been turned into a horse and carried the soldiers' victuals about in a sack. This had truly happened as he recorded it, yet seemed it but a dream unto him.

This is a most remarkable happening and we can only regret that St Augustine does not give us more details. Yet the story was told to him by the son of the man to whom it happened, which leads me to suppose that it is true. Hence the drugged man not only dreamed he was, but his double became projected as, a sumpter or pack-horse, in which form it laboured, outside in the real world, for the whole time he was asleep. How many of us, I wonder, undergo similar projections while we are sleeping? And of course if you forget your dreams, you will have no idea why you wake up worn out despite having slept for seven or eight hours. Perhaps being a replica pack-horse, or a hunting dog, or even a werewolf might be the answer to your morning tiredness!

If we could bring about such a projection at will, it would give us the opportunity of doing in our sleep what we could not do, for whatever reason, in our waking life. And because our physical self would be asleep in bed, we could hardly be blamed for, or found guilty of, any nefarious act committed by our animal double. We would have, in other words, the perfect alibi, although such a cover is not without its dangers.

According to the *Historia Eliensis* one of England's Anglo-Saxon queens, the notorious Aelfthryth or Elfrida, the consort of Edgar, king of the West Saxons, who ruled from AD 958 until 975, on several occasions changed her shape into that of a horse 'so that she might satisfy the unrestrainable excess of her burning lust, running and leaping hither and thither with horses, and showing herself shamelessly to them, regardless of the fear of God and the honour of the royal dignity', which sounds like fun if you're that turned on by horses. But Elfrida was caught out in her wrongdoing by none other than Byrhtnoth, the Abbot of Ely, who ducked behind a forest bush one day to empty his bowels and happened to notice Elfrida 'engaged in the preparation of magic potions' for the purpose of shape-changing, although the drugs would not have been used to physically transform her but rather to send her into a deep sleep, during the course of which she hoped to be projected in her double form as a horse.

But if Elfrida was shamed and alarmed by having her infamy witnessed, she was not bowed, and she subsequently exacted a dreadful revenge on the hapless Byrhtnoth (which was copied by Thomas Gournay and William Ogle, the assassins of the homosexual monarch Edward II) by having a red-hot sword-thong (Gournay and Ogle used a poker) thrust, via a previously inserted truncated cow's horn to prevent external burns, into his rectum and lower bowel. It was for this awful crime and for the murder, coincidentally enough, of her stepson Edward I, and perhaps for her drugged transformations into a nymphomaniacal mare, that Elfrida eventually joined a community of nuns at Wherwell, in Hampshire, 'where she passed all the remaining days of her life in grief and penitence'.

We should not be surprised at the enlargement necessary to transmogrify the double into a horse, as if it can reduce its size sufficiently to appear as a bird or a weasel, then achieving the opposite should not be too much of a problem. And anyway, because horses naturally come in a variety of sizes, it is likely that the doubles of Praestantius's father and Elfrida manifested as ponies and not as cart-horses.

There are many accounts of shape-changing in Scandinavian folk-lore and significantly most involve a particular type of warrior known as a 'berserk'. The berserks were the professional soldiers of their day; the only thing they did was fight, whereas every other man of the tribe or community was first and foremost a farmer or fisherman and only a part-time warrior. When there was no war to take part in, the berserks were essentially unemployed (although some acted as bodyguards of their chief or of the king) and sat around drinking and eating all day and generally being a drain on the community stores. They were also something of a pain because having, as they did, extremely short tempers and violently aggressive dispositions, being in their presence was like treading on eggs. They were probably, in modern terms, partially-tamed criminal psychopaths, who found a socially useful outlet for themselves as full-time warriors.

Berserks proved their worth, however, when warfare broke out, for not only were they men of enormous strength and had great skill with weapons like the battle-axe and the broadsword, but they were taken over by a unique and incompletely understood 'battle fury', given to them, they believed, by the god Odin, which enabled them to fight any enemy without fear, with the savagery of wild beasts, and without feeling pain when wounded. They also knew that victory in battle came not only through feats of valour, but by terrifying the enemy warriors beforehand, so that their courage drained away like water through sand, somewhat in the manner described below:

> They minister to their savage instincts [writes Tacitus of the Teutonic Harii] by trickery and clever timing. They black their shields and dye their bodies, and choose pitch dark nights for their battles. The shadowy, awe-inspiring appearance of such a ghoulish army inspires mortal panic; for no enemy can endure a sight so strange

and hellish. Defeat in battle always starts with the eyes. (*Germania*, 43)

Hence, given their strange psychological nature and their desire to be as fierce as possible, it is not surprising that this combination seemingly predisposed some berserks to project animal doubles with ferocious qualities, such as boars, bears, and wolves. Again, this ability was regarded as a gift of Odin, of whom it was pertinently claimed:

Odin could change himself. His body then lay as if sleeping or dead, but he became a bird or wild beast, a fish or a dragon, and journeyed in the twinkling of an eye to far-off lands, on his own errands or those of other men.

Thus the god did not physically change his shape, but projected a double of himself in the form of a bird or a beast, and to anywhere he wanted to go. And if such animal-double projection was credited to the god, it can only have derived from the actual experience of those who were his worshippers.

An account of a berserk transforming himself into an animal, by means of his double, occurs in the saga of the Danish king Hrolf. One day, it seems, Hrolf and his berserks fought against those led by king Hjorvarth, yet Hrolf's men were surprised and dismayed by the apparent absence from the battle of their greatest champion, Bothvar Bjarki. However, this was soon more than made up for by the appearance of a mysterious and frighteningly formidable bear:

King Hjorvarth and his men saw how a huge bear advanced before king Hrolf's men, and always next at hand where the king was. He killed more men with paw of his than any five of the king's champions. Blows and missiles rebounded from him, and he beat down both men and horses from king Hjorvarth's host, and everything within reach he crunched with his teeth, so that alarm and dismay arose in king Hjorvarth's host.

But despite this miraculous ursine assistance, Hrolf's men became angry that Bothvar was not fighting with them, and one of them, Hjalti, went to the king's lodging, where his shouts roused the champion from the deep sleep into which he had fallen there. Hjalti upbraided Bothvar for his cowardice, but the woken man rounded on him, saying:

> Any man else I would have killed, but now it will fare as fate would have it, that no council will serve our turn. I tell you plain truth, that I can now give the king less help in many respects than before you summoned me hence.

And indeed, when Hjalti returned to the battlefield along with Bothvar, he found that 'the bear had now vanished away from their host, and the battle was beginning to go against them'. The bear was in fact a werebear or Bothvar's animal double, which he had projected while asleep and which could only exist in its bear form while he slept.

But although the Scandinavians believed that the double (which they still call the *fylgja*; or *fulgja*, to the Teutons) could be projected as an animal having both the solidity and the ferocity of the real creature, they did not, however, generally accredit it with invulnerability like Bothvar's bear, from which blows and missiles rebounded. In fact the reverse was generally acknowledged: that the double, like the physical body, could be injured or even killed. And the injuries to one were sympathetically acquired by the other, the double's by the body, and the body's by the double; likewise, the death of one caused the death of the other.

That the double can be injured and the body, by reciprocation, is injured also, finds unexpected confirmation in the Venerable Bede's *A History of the English Church and People*.

Bede describes how an Irish monk named Fursey, who had founded a monastery at Burgh Castle, near Yarrow, in Sussex, during the reign of Sigbert, king of the East Angles (*c*. AD 633), once fell ill and lapsed into a trance 'from sunset to cockcrow'. While unconscious he underwent a double projection and found himself out of his physical body, yet in his double form, wherein he was carried, so he says, high into the sky by three angels. From that lofty position he was instructed to look below him, and on doing so he saw a gloomy valley, above which burnt four fires. These, he was told, were Falsehood, Covetousness, Discord, and Injustice, the four fires that would eventually consume the world.

As Fursey watched, the fires spread and came together into one vast conflagration, and he became frightened that he would be consumed by the blaze. The angels, however, assured him that he would suffer no harm, for being a good man who lacked the negative traits the four fires represented, it could not harm him. Yet none the less, when they parted the fire in order to return him to his body, another man's wraith, which he recognized and which was being held in the flames by devils, was thrust against him, whereby it burned him on his shoulder and jaw. This happened, the devils gloatingly told him, because he had accepted some of the man's clothing when he died, which being the property of a sinner, meant that he had to share in his punishment. And indeed, the burn marks his double received were reciprocally acquired by his physical body:

And when Fursey had been restored to his body he found that the burn that he had received in his soul had left a permanent and visible scar on his shoulder and jaw, and in this strange way his body afforded visible evidence of the inward sufferings of his soul.

Similarly, Colonel Henry Olcott, the companion for many years of the Russian mystic Madame Blavatsky, once suffered from the effects of an accidental collision that his double had had when he himself was asleep, which like the burn scar Fursey acquired from his double, likewise bears out the so-called primitive beliefs of the Scandinavians and other earlier peoples.

One morning Colonel Olcott woke up to find that his right

eye was badly bruised and he was at a complete loss to understand how such a thing could have happened, as he knew he had been neither struck in the eye by a fist nor by some object with which he had collided. He was not a sleep-walker, and anyhow, he reasoned that even if he had walked in his sleep and had bumped into something, such an accident would surely have awakened him.

However, it transpired that on the previous evening, following his departure to bed, when Madame Blavatsky and a woman friend had locked the door of their bedroom, they had observed Colonel Olcott in the room winding up a cuckoo-clock, which he normally did earlier in the evening. Because Olcott could not have accomplished this in his physical form, it seems that his double had been projected into the women's boudoir to perform the task to which habit had accustomed him. And when he examined their room, Olcott noticed a small hanging book-shelf:

one of whose shelves was of the exact height to catch my eye if I had run against it. Then there came back to me the dim recollection of myself moving towards the door from the far side of the room, with my hand outstretched as if to feel for the door, a sudden shock, the 'seeing of stars' – as it is commonly expressed – and then oblivion until morning.

The animal form taken by the double is the product of a number of factors, which include the character of the person from whom it emanates, the time of day when the projection takes place, and the activity in which it is to become involved. Some influence is also seemingly exerted by knowledge of the native fauna of the region, which means that, generally speaking, doubles don't become kangaroos in England or beavers in the Sahara desert. But perhaps understandably, and as we saw with Bothvar Bjarki, a fierce, aggressive person will tend to produce the double of a fierce and aggressive animal, which generally means one that is carnivorous, such as a wolf,

160

bear, lion, leopard, or even a crocodile, whereas someone with a more docile temperament will tend to give rise to an animal-double of a similar disposition, like a herbivorous sheep, goat, rabbit or hare, or a pony.

Folk tales and horror-story writers generally cast their fictional fiends as creatures of the night, and they have good reason for doing this, aside from the fact that it is dark then. For it is during the night that we sleep, and it is during sleep, as we know, that the double can most easily leave the body. And if it manifests as an animal, this will naturally be one that is familiar with the night and can function in darkness, like a wolf, cat, bat, or an owl, which are better known to writers of horror as a werewolf, werecat, werebat or vampire, and wereowl.

We know that certain lunar phases have a destabilizing effect on the human psyche and upon our emotions. This is most noticeable at full moon, when there is a well-authenticated upsurge in violent crime, car accidents, suicide, mental breakdown, rape, rioting, and domestic quarrels, although such activities also increase, but to a lesser extent, at new moon and at first and second quarter moons. Such an unsettling effect is naturally felt by the sleeper, who is more likely to project a double then than at other times, and if he does, one of an animal, whose type will be determined by those factors mentioned above. This of course explains why werewolves and vampires, as well as other were-animals, are specifically linked with the full moon. I know that my own sleep is always disturbed on the night of the full moon, even though I may not be aware the moon is full that night, which speaks eloquently of its power to discombobulate us, although I have not yet found myself running in wolf form (or any other animal form) through the local woods then. I do, however, look forward to the experience should it ever occur.

Werewolves have a long history and, strangely, a special appeal to Europeans, despite the fact that most of us have never seen a real wolf, which has been hunted to extinction throughout much of the European continent. In Britain, the aforementioned King Edgar, second husband of the notorious Elfrida, 'tooke order for the destroying of them throughout the whole realm', and he issued a decree forcing the Welsh, in whose kingdom the last of the wolves had taken refuge, to kill three hundred of them each year and send him their heads in lieu of a money tribute. The Welsh were so happy to pay the tribute in wolves, that by the end of the fourth year there were none left to decapitate. And Englishmen of the time loved to call themselves after wolves, and many were variously known, curiously enough, as 'Old Wolf', or 'Noble Wolf', or 'Industrious Wolf', or 'Prosperous Wolf', which in their Anglo-Saxon tongue were respectively pronounced as Ealdwulf, Ethelwulf, Berthwulf, and Eadwulf. Beowulf, the hero of the poem bearing his name, is a contraction of Baedowulf, meaning 'War Wolf'.

The belief in werewolves dates back at least as far as fifth century BC, for Herodotus, writing in *The Histories*, remarks of the Neuri, a Scythian tribe inhabiting what is now the Russian province of Belarus, that 'once a year every Neurian turns into a wolf for a day or two, and then turns back into a man again. Of course, I do not believe this tale; all the same, they tell it, and even swear to the truth of it'. However, had Herodotus known that the Neurians did not mean they physically changed into wolves but rather projected their doubles in a wolf form, he might not have been so dismissive of their claims. It may well be that the Neuri were aided in their double projection by ingesting a special drug, perhaps during an annual religious ceremony, one similar in its effects to that swallowed by the father of Praestantius, and which would certainly account for the 'day or two' time length of their vulpine experience.

Similarly, it was said that each year an Arcadian shepherd was turned into a wolf. The Arcadians were the most backward of the Greek tribes and their oxymoronic civilizer was Lycaon, whose name means 'Deluding Wolf', probably because, having sacrificed a boy to Zeus, he was changed into a wolf as punishment. Later, Lycaon's sons were foolish enough to not only murder one of their brothers, but to serve up his guts to Zeus, in the form of umble soup, at a banquet attended by the god. Supernaturally perceiving what was placed before him, the disgusted and angry deity flung away the soup and changed all the sons, of whom there were fifty, into wolves, with the exception of the one forming an ingredient in the soup, whom he restored to life in his human form.

But despite Zeus's revulsion at such cannibalistic practices, the Arcadians continued to sacrifice a boy to the god for centuries afterwards. As part of the annual ritual, portions of the human victim's intestines were mixed with those taken from other animals to make more umble soup, and the whole revolting pottage was set before some shepherds, who were obliged to eat it. This was an alfresco meal, swallowed on the banks of a stream. The shepherd, it was said, who ate the boy's guts soon afterwards began to howl like a wolf – then he threw off his clothes, splashed across the stream, and ran into the open country beyond, where he ironically, being a shepherd, became transformed into a werewolf. If he then avoided eating human flesh for eight years, he would at the end of that lengthy period regain his human shape and, by recrossing the stream and putting back on his clothes, rejoin human society.

If we are expected to believe that the shepherd physically changed into a wolf, then we are right to reject the whole saga as impossible. Yet the reader might have noticed that the report has an underlying similarity to those recounting the emergence of doubles as were-animals mentioned earlier, notably the ingestion by the shepherd of a soporific meal – the eating of entrails was the only meat dish available to the agricultural poor, who naturally gorged themselves when the opportunity arose – and the subsequent crossing of a stream, which in itself is symbolic of sleep and dreaming (Abba fans may remember the line 'I crossed the stream, I had a dream'). Hence one goes over to the other side in a dream, which is partnered in reality by the slipping out from one's physical self of the double as a were-animal, in this case a wolf, through whose eyes the dream apparently takes place.

Eight years is likewise an impossibly long time for anyone to remain as a werewolf, especially if the creature is a transformed double, yet if we read this as a typical ancient exaggeration of what in reality was eight days, we obtain a meaningful connection with the moon, for the Greeks sacrificed to Selene, the moon goddess, on the eighth day of each lunation – at first quarter moon – when as I have already pointed out there is a general unsettling of the human mind and thus a greater likelihood of were-animal projection. And if human intestines perchance contain a somniferous drug, a blackout lasting eight days may well have been the result of eating them in umble soup – which is suggested by the derivation of *umble* from 'numbles' (meaning deer's entrails), whose cognate may be 'numb', meaning 'deprived of feeling or the power of motion'.

The gross behaviour of Lycaon and his sons, fabulous though it seems, is made doubly interesting because it persuaded Zeus that the whole of mankind was unfit to inhabit the earth, and he therefore resolved to destroy everybody by means of a global inundation, which became known as Deucalion's flood, because Deucalion and his wife Pyrrha, like Noah and his unnamed wife, managed to survive it by building an ark. Hence werewolves were involved, in an inverse way, in the submergence of the world.

Further, the reader may recall that Noah, the hero of the Biblical deluge, had three sons Ham, Shem and Japhet, who became, with their wives, the respective progenitors of the new populations of Africa, Europe, and Asia. Thus according to Biblical tradition every European can claim descent from Shem, every African from Ham, and every Asian from Japhet.

In accordance with this tradition, the people of Turkistan, the Moguls or Mongols, believe they originate from Japhet or Japhet Khan, as they call him. They say too that their tenth king by descent was Yuldooz Khan, who ruled over them following their migration from the mountains to the plains below.

The Double as Were-animal

Now Yuldooz Khan had a beautiful granddaughter named Alankooah, who was married at the age of fourteen, but who, unhappily for her, was widowed and left childless before she reached her eighteenth birthday. But not long afterwards, while she was still in mourning, Alankooah was one night surprised by a ray of light that entered the window of her hut and brightly illuminated its interior. The light then condensed (or collapsed in upon itself) to generate the form of a handsome young man, who forcibly took advantage of the frightened woman, despite all her attempts to resist him. And after he had had his way with her, the young man changed his shape into that of a wolf, and in this guise left her. The surprise visitation and its vulpine aftermath was repeated and continued until Alankooah became pregnant, notwithstanding the attempts of her shocked relatives to destroy the unwanted lover. Alankooah eventually gave birth to male triplets, one of whom became the ancestor of all the later kings of Turkistan.

What is particularly noteworthy about this ancient story is that the descendants of the Moguls in Turkistan do not know who or what the 'man of light', as they call him, was. Some say he was an angel, others that he was the light of Allah, although these are speculations as opposed to what in other circumstances would be religious certainty. The story, however, finds an almost exact parallel in the conception of Merlin, whose mother, a nun, was visited in her cell by a phantom man. Such uncertainty in itself suggests the reality of the event, which while incredible does find an explanation in the projection of a double, which is sometimes accompanied by a light, and which would allow it to miraculously enter Alankooah's bedroom, where it was able, like the double of Ariston, to engage in sexual intercourse and so impregnate Alankooah. And of course by afterwards changing itself into a werewolf, the double not only adopted what may be one of its natural animal-forms, but seemingly confirms what I have been arguing is the most likely explanation for were-animals, that is, they result from the transformation of the double rather than from the impossible transmogrification of the physical body.

An allied explanation for were-animals is less plausible. This postulates that once the soul has left the physical body, which normally occurs when the body is asleep or in a trance or a similar cataleptic condition, it then enters the dead body of an animal like a wolf and reanimates it. Presumably the resurrected animal must be recently dead, for not only is it difficult to imagine how a corpse with rigor mortis can be prompted into running about again, but there are no accounts that I am aware of which state that were-animals with rotting, fly-blown flesh have been seen roaming the countryside. Of course we know that modern science can revivify dead people, whose souls are drawn back into their bodies when resuscitation occurs, and it is possible therefore to imagine how a wandering double could enter a freshly dead, but perhaps not too dead, wolf corpse and so reanimate it. And while unlikely, it would explain why werewolves are no longer seen in Britain, for without wolves in the wild, there can be no wolf corpses for vulpinely-inclined doubles to revivify. Dead foxes would seem to be a suitable alternative, although in many areas, particularly those near cities, domestic cat corpses are more readily available, which may explain why strange felines like the Beast of Exmoor, the East Sussex Panther, the Surrey Puma, the Kidderminster Jungle Cat, and the Finchley Lynx, have been spotted on many occasions, but never caught!

The transfer of a human soul into the body of an animal is known as 'metempsychosis'. This is usually regarded as happening after a person dies, although it would seem most convenient and plausible for the freed soul to then enter and inhabit the developing foetus of a wolf, cat or whatever, rather than to improbably revivify a dead adult animal. For if it can do that, then why can't it revivify its own dead self? Metempsychosis, a variant of reincarnation, is an ancient belief. The ancient Greek philosopher Empedocles, for example, was so sure that he had previously existed as a boy, a girl, a beast, a bird, and a sea fish, that he became convinced he was living through his last incarnation. And to speed up his soul's escape from the world, he committed suicide in 430 BC by flinging himself into the fiery volcanic cone of Mount Etna, whose upwelling of heated air he hoped would carry his soul to the realm of the gods.

However, it may be that the double is not always able to fully transform itself into an animal, or indeed even want to. In this regard it is relevant to note that there are many accounts of witnessed man-like creatures, which seem real enough to those who see them but which cannot be subsequently tracked down or identified. Such beings may be temporary, quasi-physical double-forms, whose sudden return to the person from whom they originate would account for their mysterious ability to vanish without trace. One of the most ancient and interesting of such creatures is the satyr, a beast with the body of a man and the legs of a goat, very muscular and hairy, and with a strong sex drive. There were several sightings of these improbable animals in rural spots in ancient times, and one was reportedly captured near the town of Durresi in what is now Albania, prior to the embarkation of the Roman army led by Lucius Cornelius Sylla from there, in 84 BC. It unfortunately did not understand what was said to it, and the sounds it made, writes Plutarch, were quite unintelligible to its Roman captors, being 'something between the neighing of a horse and the bleating of a goat'.

However, a satyr was seen much more recently, on Mount Parnassus in Greece, by Charles Seltman, afterwards Lecturer in Classical Archaeology in the University of Cambridge, a highly reputable and reliable witness, in April 1925. His description of what he saw has all the hallmarks of an encounter with a were-animal, notably in regard to the strange disappearance of the creature, although I none the less would not like to categorically state that satyrs do not physically exist.

Seltman and his wife, accompanied by two colleagues and a Greek guide, had climbed some 4000 feet up the sacred mountain and, after refreshing themselves with a drink from a cold spring, had turned eastwards across the upland plateau; their subsequent progress was made somewhat slow by tiredness and by conversation, although Seltman himself stepped out and soon gained on the rest. He writes:

> Before long I found myself walking far ahead of the other four; half a mile in advance of them; silent, no distinct thoughts, but the mystic, the numinous taking possession of my being.
>
> And then suddenly I saw HIM . . . matted black hair, long pointed ears, a sturdy muscular body deep red-brown of tan, hairy, and still more hairy where the thighs began to be merged into goat-legs ending in hooves. A black tail; I took it all in as he trotted across my path not twenty yards away. I stopped and he stopped, and both looked at one another. Never have I seen such fear in eyes except, perhaps, in the eyes of a trembling spaniel. Suddenly he drummed on his chest with clenched fists, turned and ran straight for the trunk of a large cedar. Filled now with delight and curiosity I walked silently and as quickly as I dared up to that tree and round it. No satyr to be seen. That was a reality.

We must regret that Mr Seltman did not run to that tree, although even had he done so he might not have seen more of the satyr, for it probably vanished by being instantaneously taken back into the body of a Greek goatherd, lying somewhere below in the shade of an olive tree, snoring sonorously as in his dream he roamed the mountainside in the form he subconsciously felt himself to be, half-man, half-goat, wherein he was temporarily freed from the social and sexual restrictions of his waking existence, until by ill luck he crossed the path of some damned outsider, who sent him fleeing in fear of discovery, exposure and disgrace. What a relief it was to suddenly wake up and find out it was only a foolish dream!

I felt younger, lighter, happier in body; within I was conscious of a heady recklessness, a current of disordered sensual images running like a mill-race in my fancy, a solution of the bonds of obligation, an unknown but not an innocent freedom of the soul. I knew myself, at the first breath of this new life, to be more wicked, tenfold more wicked, sold a slave to my original evil; and the thought, in that moment, braced and delighted me like wine.

We can imagine how these words, or ones very like them, might have been written by the man who produced that satyr, or indeed by anyone who has found himself or herself in the double-form of an animal. For by becoming an animal, or half an animal, one is loosened from those restraints imposed by civilization and human upbringing, and allowed, in a very real and direct way, to experience not wickedness, as Robert Louis Stevenson interpreted the joyful, untrammelled feelings above of Mr Hyde, but contact with the core of ourselves, with unmodified nature, with the edge that meets hidden edges, that lie lost in the darkness which blinds our civilized eyes.

8 The Second Self Examined

I saw the figure of a lovely maid
Seated alone beneath a darksome tree . . .
The bright corporeal presence, form, and face,
Remaining still distinct, grew thin and rare,
Like sunny mist; at length the golden hair,
Shape, limbs, and heavenly features, keeping pace
Each, with the other, in a lingering race
Of dissolution, melted into air.
    From *Ecclesiastical Sketches* by William Wordsworth

The very number and overall similarity of the accounts of doubles and the circumstances in which they have appeared, suggest that the double is an authentic phenomenon and not the product of mistaken identity, faulty observation, disturbed minds, over-active imaginations, excessive indulgence in drink or drugs, or downright lying. Yet despite their long history and evident genuineness, doubles have been largely ignored as a subject for paranormal and scientific research, which is both curious and disturbing, particularly in view of their relatively common occurrence.

However, the double or *doppelgänger* is an entity of some contradiction, being at once familiar and unfamiliar, an apparent enigma. It will therefore be helpful to review its main characteristics and properties and to note again those which show some variance. This may in turn allow us to determine the double's nature and purpose, and further, to

170

decide if it is the same as, or different from, the astral body and the ghost.

We can be confident in asserting, I believe, that the human double normally resides within our living physical body and conforms to it both externally and internally. Hence in this regard the double is the body's exact counterpart or likeness, although it does project slightly from its surface to form the surrounding aura. The latter is transparent but can none the less be faintly seen.

On occasion, however, the double can separate itself from the body, when it may be directly projected to, or made to manifest in, a distant place. How such projection occurs is presently unknown. The double's departure from the body can happen when the person is either awake or asleep (or otherwise unconscious), although it more often occurs during the latter periods.

Double projection may also happen during religious ecstasy, when the affected person is awake yet in a state of mystical consciousness. Such separation is signified by the word ecstasy itself, which is formed from the Greek root *eksto* meaning 'I detach' or 'I burst out'. When a person dies the entity that leaves the body is called the wraith; it consists of the double and the consciousness.

The double can be seen by others when it is apart from the body, and such witnesses invariably report that it is indistinguishable from the real person. Indeed, it is typically mistaken for him until it either mysteriously disappears or the subject gives proof that he was elsewhere at the time. Yet curiously, the double can sometimes be seen by one person and not by another; or it may be visible to others but, oddly, not to the person from whom it originates. Hence the perception of the double may depend partly at least on the psychic sensitivity of those who see it.

The double is typically paler in colouring than the real person, and while it is otherwise normally an exact likeness, clothes and all, of him, it may, on occasion, be dressed in replicas of different clothes and of different jewellery and other ornaments. Sometimes its hair colour, or its apparent age, may vary as well; it can also be of a different size, or even have a completely different appearance. Indeed, there is some evidence to suggest that the double can, in rare instances, take on the form of an animal. In its human form it often carries doubles of those objects, like umbrellas, briefcases, and hand-bags, which are being carried by its physical source. And it may sometimes, although again rarely, be seen driving a dou-ble of its car or riding a replica bicycle.

Although the double may sometimes spontaneously leave the body and wander around on its own for no obvious rea-son, it is typically projected from the body by strong, often negative emotions, like stress, anxiety, or apprehension at the approach of death. But equally, an earnest need or desire to be elsewhere, or a concern for the plight of another or oth-ers, can bring double projection about. The time it spends away from the body varies depending upon the purpose of its absence, but separations lasting longer than three hours are probably rare, unless of course the person is asleep, when they may potentially be much longer. Relatively brief separa-tions of under half an hour, however, are probably most usual.

But while the double looks real, its apparent solidity is variable. On occasion, for example, it may lack any sem-blance of substance whatsoever, the exploratory hand passing unresistingly through it. More often, however, it demon-strates some slight resistance or power to impede, one similar to that offered by crepe paper or fine muslin. Yet most com-monly and curiously, the double mimics the impenetrability of ordinary flesh and blood and hence feels exactly like the living person. The double can also manipulate matter in the same way that its source can, by opening doors or cupboards, by lifting cups and books, by ringing bells, and by turning keys, etc. This means that, along with substance, it also has sufficient strength both to grip and to overcome the force of gravity and the inertia of the handled object. Its essential solidity is also revealed by its observed inability to pass like a ghost through walls, doors and other solid barriers.

The double is sometimes conscious, sometimes not. When it separates from someone who is awake, it is usually lacking in this regard, the consciousness remaining in the person concerned, who is normally quite unaware that his double has left his body. Without consciousness the double is unable to speak. Yet sometimes it can show awareness by looking at those who see it, by moving its lips, and even by saying a sentence or two, which suggests it is not entirely lacking in consciousness. By contrast, a double that leaves the body of someone who is asleep or in a trance or a coma usually departs with his consciousness and is thereby able to have rational (and sometimes long) conversations with the people it meets. Also, a sleeping person will often view the world through the eyes of his wandering double, although he regards what he sees as a dream. This in turn probably means that a telepathic connection develops between the consciousness of the double and that remaining in the brain of the sleeping individual. But none the less, even conscious doubles are naturally taciturn and usually avoid entering into conversation with real people.

The double's ability to speak and behave as the real person indicates that it has a duplicated internal structure as well as his or her external form. This must certainly be true if we can accept those rare cases when a double reportedly has sexual intercourse with an ordinary person, whom it may either impregnate or be impregnated by. Indeed, the ancient and widespread belief in the incubus and succubus, which are supposed evil spirits that sexually force themselves upon, respectively, sleeping women and sleeping men, may have arisen from such instances. The double's quasi-physical nature is further suggested by the fact that it can be injured, perhaps even killed, while its reciprocal connection with the physical body means that the latter sympathetically acquires the double's injuries or dies from its fatal ones. Moreover, when a person's consciousness is in the separated double, he often thinks he is still inside his body, which implies that his double shares many of his body's internal characteristics (so that it feels, in other words, the same).

Yet if the double is quasi-physical, we don't unfortunately know if the physical portion consists of ordinary atoms and molecules, in perhaps a more rarefied or tenuous state, or if it is composed of some physico-chemical variant, like a plasma. The remainder of the double may be spiritual in nature, whatever that means exactly.

We likewise do not know how the double is able to vanish from sight, and when it does, how it is able to retain its integrity, or for that matter how it is able to project itself directly to a particular place, which may be many miles away from its human source. These are properties or capabilities that seemingly belong more to spirit than to matter, and if so naturally indicate that the double does contain a spiritual component. This concurs with the ancient Egyptian belief that the double is part material and part spiritual.

The above-mentioned characteristics of the double are fully shared by the wraith, which is the name given to the double when it leaves the body of a person who is dying and which persists for some time after his death. The wraith has the same degree of substance or solidity and the same inherent strength, which allows it to manipulate matter when required, and partnered as it is by the dead person's consciousness, it is also able to speak.

However, the double cannot, as we have seen, remain apart from the living body for very long, and hence it cannot take up an independent existence of its own. This is presumably because, being a quasi-physical entity, it has energy requirements like the body. These are normally satisfied by the foods we eat, as each different food type, according to the ancient Egyptians, contains a double of itself, whose energy is available to the body's double. Yet when the double separates from the body, its energy needs not only become greater, but as it cannot masticate and digest ordinary foods, which contain the double forms upon which it lives, it must depend on its own limited energy resources. The double is apparently unable to drink ordinary liquids either; the only instance of a drinking double that I came across was that of Alexander Ferguson, the lunatic. These energy factors necessarily curtail the length of the double's excursions.

But the double normally only leaves the body when it is forced out, so to speak, by some demanding emotional state like anxiety, fear, concern, or frustrated love, or when the person to whom it belongs wants desperately to be with, or know about, some absent loved one, or by the approach of his or her death. Thus in life it seemingly functions as an emergency communicative mechanism, enabling the person to make direct contact with another or others at a distance. It simply did not evolve to be a separate, independent system.

However, when the double separates from someone who is awake it is usually unaccompanied by his consciousness, so that it lacks awareness and is mute, and thus behaves, to all intents and purposes, like a zombie. Yet it can nevertheless still perform a contacting role in that state by simply showing itself, thereby telling those who are anxiously awaiting, say, the real person's arrival, that he is on his way and will be there soon. This is sometimes inaccurately known as an arrival premonition. And for those adepts who can project their doubles at will, the double can be used, as we have seen, to lure pursuers into taking the wrong route so as to give the real person the opportunity to escape. The appearance of the mute double can also alert others when the real person is in danger, while the wraith may perform a similar rousing function when its physical self has died. Furthermore, the mute double sometimes acts as a herald of death, by either appearing to the person who is going to die, who in effect sees himself, or to those who know and love him. In both cases a warning is received, which may help those concerned to face, or accept, the inevitable.

There have been a number of attempts over the years to weigh the double, or at least the wraith, by carefully measuring any drop in weight at the moment of a person's death. The difference determined is invariably very small, with ear-

175

lier studies reporting a weight loss of between two and three ounces, whereas similar research done in 1993 by a team from Berlin's Technical University, led by Dr Becker Mertens, who weighed 200 terminally ill German patients just before and after they died, found that the average loss in weight was no more than 1/3,000 of an ounce. Yet against this virtually weightless figure must be set the impressions of people who have been sat on or lain on by wraiths, who invariably report that they are surprisingly heavy, to the extent that in some instances they seem to weigh more than the dead person! In one famous case in Buckinghamshire, reported by William of Newburgh, the wraith of a recently dead man one night visited his widow and 'not only terrified her on awaking, but nearly crushed her by the insupportable weight of his body'. And I can still recall the night when I woke up to find the wraith of my Pyrenean mountain dog lying beside me, which felt just as solid and as heavy as she did when alive.

Astral projection differs from the projection of the double in that whatever leaves the body is invisible to onlookers. Also anyone undergoing astral projection is always conscious of what is happening and of being outside his body, and while he is sometimes aware of still having his bodily form, which he may be able to see, not only is he unable to affect his surroundings in any way and can pass unhindered, like a ghost, through walls and doors, but he may find he has another form altogether, such as a point of light or even a geometrical shape. These differences indicate that while astral projection, like double projection, is an out-of-body experience, it is essentially a departure of the consciousness from the body. However, the two phenomena are necessarily combined when a conscious double (or wraith) is projected, because this unites the quasi-physical likeness with the consciousness.

But if some people – although no more than a tiny minority – are seen long after death as ghosts, what relationship do ghosts bear to wraiths? A ghost does of course have the dead person's external likeness, but none the less it lacks the substance that doubles and wraiths possess, which explains why it can pass through walls and doors without hindrance and can appear and disappear just as readily. A ghost has no replica internal organs, which is why they rarely, if ever, say anything – those that do are almost certainly wraiths. They are likewise devoid of consciousness, so they have no awareness of what they are doing and their behaviour lacks point or purpose. Indeed, they tend to manifest at random, frighten whoever sees them, and then vanish without trace until the next time. But because they only have to sustain an external likeness their energy requirements are considerably less than the double, which is why they can persist for much longer, although even the oldest ghosts date back no more than two or three hundred years. Such geriatric apparitions, however, are rare; most ghosts are much younger. Ghost-spotters have noticed that as time goes by ghosts not only become hazier in appearance but also manifest less frequently, which is what we would expect to happen if their energy stores are gradually being used up.

These characteristics suggest that the ghost, rather than being a spiritual entity, is a diminished version of the quasi-physical double (or wraith), being even more tenuous, although it can appear just as lifelike and real. The ghost may therefore be a wraith that has either run down its energy battery, so that only the appearance of the double remains or, as seems more likely, one whose outer form or likeness was left behind like a cast-off skin when the wraith was projected into the next dimension at death. This latter notion accords with the teaching of Lucretius, who theorized that 'replicas or insubstantial shapes of things are thrown off from the surface of objects. These we must denote as an outer skin or film, because each particular floating image wears the aspect and form of the object from whose body it has emanated'.

In this regard it is relevant to point out that most ghosts originate from people who have been brutally murdered, while the remainder are either the apparitions of suicide victims or, as happens sometimes, those killed in tragic accidents. It is certainly true that people who have died happily do not give rise to ghosts. Murders, however, are invariably accompanied by the expression of very negative emotions. Hatred, lust, jealousy, greed, or rage, for example, may motivate the perpetrators, while suicides are frequently driven to the edge by self-loathing, depression or despair. And fear, shock and anger are felt by murder victims and by those who die in accidents. Such strong emotions may act like a rasp and strip away the outer layer of the victim's wraith, so that its semblance remains behind as a ghost to haunt the room, house or spot where the death occurred for as long as the negative emotions hold it there or until the spectre loses all its energy and vanishes of its own accord. The rest of the wraith form, however, is projected across the divide that separates this world from the next, so that it enters, in other words, 'that undiscovered country from whose bourne no traveller returns' – as Shakespeare somewhat erroneously put it.

The projection of the wraith after bodily death explains why so many of the accounts of life in the next world given by spiritualists and psychics, and by those who have had a near-death experience, reveal that the dead still have their recognizable human forms, that they wear similar clothes, and that they generally comport themselves in much the same way as they did in life. What the psychics and others have seen or met are projected wraiths, which means that, as each wraith possesses its original consciousness, they are essentially the same people both in appearance and in every other way. This is why they still want and need to eat, to sleep, to talk, to flirt and to make love, which they can do as well in their double form as they previously could in their full physical form, when they were, as we mistakenly say, 'still alive'.

But here we arrive at an apparent conundrum, for if whatever injury done to the body reciprocally affects the double, and vice versa, why doesn't the death of the body likewise kill off the wraith?

The answer lies in noting that despite the ancients occasional witnessing of doubles and wraiths with injuries identical to those sustained by their physical counterparts, which suggested such reciprocity to them, they would none the less never have seen a dead double. Rather, when a person died his double was never seen again, which is quite different, although its absence would naturally have suggested to them that it too had died. But of course the double (or wraith) wouldn't be seen again if it was projected to somewhere away from the earth, perhaps even into another dimension of being, in which case its death would be apparent rather than actual.

Although we don't know where wraiths are projected to, we can reasonably postulate that they don't immediately go to heaven (if there is such a place). The wraith, after all, is interim in nature, being half-way between the physicality of this world and the incorporeality of the next. Its function therefore is to hold the consciousness (which is the real 'I' of a person) in a recognizable and familiar boundary and setting, which allows it to come to terms with not only the demise of its physical body but also to prepare itself for whatever lies ahead of it. The future alternatives for it are or include:

1 The return of itself to earth, by being born into another physical body, either that of a person or an animal (respectively known as reincarnation and metempsychosis);
2 Some form of punishment or re-education for its sins committed while in the body, followed perhaps by its rebirth;
3 Its movement into some higher and wholly spiritual realm (which is commonly called 'heaven').

It is probable that the first of these is the commonest alternative, each of us having to live through a multitude of earthly lives before we acquire sufficient sense and goodness to be allowed to proceed further, although many will have to undergo some sort of punishment or awareness-raising before even metempsychosis is allowed. And while reincarnation is popularly regarded as an imported eastern concept, it was widely known and accepted in ancient Egypt and Greece, and among the Romans. Its essence and purpose is delightfully expressed by John Masefield in his poem entitled *A Creed*, which begins:

> *I held that when a person dies*
> *His soul returns again to earth;*
> *Arrayed in some new flesh-disguise*
> *Another mother gives him birth.*
> *With sturdier limbs and brighter brain*
> *The old soul takes the road again . . .*
>
> *. . . And as I wander on the roads*
> *I shall be helped and healed and blessed;*
> *Dear words shall cheer and be as goads*
> *To urge to heights before unguessed.*
> *The road shall be the road I made;*
> *All that I gave shall be repaid.*
>
> *So shall I fight, so shall I tread,*
> *In this long war beneath the stars;*
> *So shall a glory wreathe my head,*
> *So shall I faint and show the scars,*
> *Until this case, this clogging mould,*
> *Be smithied all to kingly gold.*

However, everyone should expect to remain as a wraith for many earth years, as one of the wraith's other-worldly responsibilities is to greet those of loved ones who die later, so that they do not find themselves either alone or among strangers when they arrive. Parents, for example, may predecease their children by thirty or more years, and so we would expect a delay of at least that long before they are free to move on to one or other of the situations mentioned above. Yet this is not to say that time passes with the equivalent slowness in the domain of the wraith as it does here on earth. For while time, to a wraith, may seemingly pass by at the same rate, it will actually go by much more slowly than it does here, so that one day there might equal, for example, one of our years.

The notion of the wraith as a temporary receptacle for the consciousness accords with what many ancient religions believed about the afterlife. The Greeks, for example, said that the souls of the dead go first to the Asphodel Fields, where they continue to live much as they had done on earth, although it was pictured as a rather dark and gloomy spot, lying under the earth. Then, after judgement, a soul might be reborn on earth (as the Pythagoreans and others believed), or punished by being sent to Tartarus, or rewarded by being allowed into Elysium, where all is sunshine, revelry, and happiness. Because the punishments were given to the quasi-physical souls or wraiths, they could be just as nasty as those meted out on earth, which is why Tantalus was tormented with hunger and thirst and Sisyphus was made to roll a rock endlessly up a hill. A wraith, like the physical body, can be hurt by being burned or beaten or whatever.

Modern Catholics likewise believe that the dead are first taken to a neutral holding area, which they call purgatory, from where they are subsequently dispatched, depending on how they lived their lives on earth, either to heaven or to hell. Most Christians also believe, like Tertullian, that what departs from the body at death is the soul or spirit, which has 'the human form, the same as its body, only it is delicate, clear, and ethereal' (Bain). This description accords with the spiritual portion of the wraith, which suggests that the two are synonymous. Yet our individuality after death lasts only as long as our consciousness remains in our wraith. Hence if we are not reborn, then once the wraith form ceases to be, our individual consciousness moves on to become part of the Universal Consciousness, wherein all awareness of a personal identity is lost in the same way that a glass of water is lost when it is emptied into a river. Yet in the loss there is of course the gain of so much more! This is the equivalent of what we like to call heaven.

Doubles

The wraith can be sustained for the equivalent of many earth years because in the holding area to which it is projected, which we may term the Asphodel Fields, purgatory or whatever, it has access to injestible food doubles, which may originate from those foods that weren't eaten on earth, just as it can wear or use the similarly projected doubles of clothes, tooth-brushes, books and so on, which may or may not once have been its own.

The projection of the wraith at death is sometimes seen, albeit rarely. Yet we do find several accounts of such witnessed passings over in the writings of the early church fathers, whose descriptions, for long ignored as mere pious and over-imaginative depictions of supposed transitions, may well be accurate.

In his *Life of Cuthbert*, for example, the Venerable Bede recounts how the saint (AD 634–687), while on a visit to the monastery of the holy virgin Aelfflaed, fell into a trance at dinner. 'His limbs went limp and useless, his face changed colour, his eyes became fixed in amazement, and the knife fell from his hand on to the table,' notes the author. When Cuthbert came to himself again, Aelfflaed asked him what he witnessed in his vision, and he told her that 'I saw the soul of some holy man being borne by the hands of angels into the joy of Heaven'. And indeed it was later discovered that at the moment of his vision one of the monastery's shepherds, a good and honest man, had died by falling out of a tree.

And similarly, when writing about the death of Hilda, the abbess of the monastery of Whitby, in Yorkshire, who passed over during the morning of 17 November 680, Bede says that one of her nuns 'saw her soul ascend to heaven in the company of angels' before she knew Hilda was dead; while that evening, at the monastery at Hackness, founded by Hilda and lying about fifteen miles away to the south, a nun named Begu witnessed the roof of her dormitory apparently open, letting in a great light, wherein she likewise 'saw the soul of God's servant Hilda borne up to heaven in the midst of the light accompanied and guided by angels'. And again, Begu's vision happened before news of Hilda's death had reached Hackness.

The phrase 'borne up to heaven' is a euphemism meaning only that the wraiths were moving sky-wards; neither Cuthbert nor the nuns knew where they were being taken, but simply assumed it was to paradise. But fortunately, however, we have a later account left by a man who underwent, like the previously mentioned Fursey, a long double projection and whose experiences conveniently fill out the rest of the story for us.

This strange adventure happened to a French monk named Sauve (later canonized), who one day fell into a lethargy or death-like trance at the monastery where he was abbot. His fellow monks, believing him to be dead, put him into a coffin and prepared to celebrate his funeral rites. However, before the coffin lid was closed and screwed down Sauve was seen to move, and he was immediately and joyfully taken back to his bed, where he gradually recovered, although he remained speechless for three days; he also refused to take any food or drink. Then, on the third day, he came to himself sufficiently to summon his fellow monks to his bedside. He described to them, to their amazement, what had happened to him when he was apparently no longer alive.

> I was carried upwards into the sky by angels (he recounted), from where it seemed to me that I had beneath my feet not only this muddy earth, but also the sun and the moon, the clouds and the stars; the angels led me through a doorway more brilliant than the day into a house filled by an ineffable light, wherein there was a floor resplendent with gold and silver; this was covered by so great a multitude of people of both sexes, that one could see across neither the length nor the breadth of the crowd. When the angels that preceded me had made a path through the throng, we arrived at a place that we had already seen from afar and above which was suspended a cloud brighter than all light; we could not dis-

183

tinguish either the sun or the moon, or any star, and it shone by its own brightness; from within the cloud came a voice resembling the sound of mighty waters ... standing at the place the angels indicated, I was suffused with a perfume of exquisite sweetness, which nourished me in such a way that I felt no more hunger or thirst. I heard the voice say: 'He may return to earth, for he is necessary to the churches'. I heard only the voice, because we could not see him who spoke ... having then left my companions, I descended in tears, and left where I had entered.

The place where Sauve's wraith was taken certainly sounds as if it was a temporary holding area, perhaps a part of purgatory, where the wraiths, of which there were evidently many thousands, remain until their next move is decided upon or until their job of greeting following family members and loved ones is accomplished.

And thus must I now leave you where I began, with the comforting message that you are not alone. Within you lies your double, temporarily trapped though it may be, yet poised to move on to greater and more marvellous things when your physical body, so to speak, gives up the ghost. It has probably gone on some rambles while you have been asleep, perhaps even while you are awake. You may even remember one or two. It is of course just marking time in your physical body, which is no more important to, or representative of, yourself than your car is, and just as you change your car for a new model from time to time, so your wraith or conscious double, which is the real you, will move to a new body when the present one croaks it – if you can't escape, that is, the tiresome treadmill of punishment and rebirth.

But if you would like to get off the treadmill, then take a careful look at your morals and motives. If all you care about is money, power and yourself, then like Arnold Schwarzenegger, you'll be back; but if there's a fair measure of love and kindness in your heart, you stand a good chance of being finally set free, and of leaving the physical world behind you – to become part of the Universal Consciousness, which the wise call God.

Bibliography

Apparitions, Supernatural Occurrences, Demonstrative of the Soul's Immortality, etc. (J. Barker, 1799)

Aubrey, John, *Miscellanies Upon Various Subjects* (John Russell Smith, 1857)

Augustine, Saint, *The City of God* [trans. John Healey] (Everyman's Library, 1945)

Bain, Alexander, *Mind and Body* (Henry S. King & Co., 1873)

Baring-Gould, Sabine, *A Book of Folk-Lore* (W. Collins Sons & Co.)

Baring-Gould, Sabine, *The Book of Were-Wolves: Being an Account of a Terrible Superstition* (Smith, Elder and Co., 1865)

Baxter, Richard, *The Certainty of the World of the Spirits Fully Evinced* (Joseph Smith, 1834)

Bede, *A History of the English Church and People* [trans. Leo Sherley-Price] (Penguin Classics, 1955)

Bramley-Moore, Zelma, *Strange Diary* (Rider & Co.,1937)

Brittan, Dr S. B., *Man and his Relations* (W.A. Townsend and Adams, 1868)

Burton, Robert, *The Anatomy of Melancholy* (Everyman's Library, J.M. Dent & Sons, 1932)

Creighton, Helen, *Bluenose Ghosts* (McGraw-Hill Ryerson, 1976)

Crowe, Catherine, *The Night-Side of Nature* (The Aquarian Press, 1986)

Davidson, H.R. Ellis, *Gods and Myths of Northern Europe* (Penguin Books, 1974)

Davies, Rodney, *Discover Your Psychic Powers* (The Aquarian Press, 1992)

Davies, Rodney, *Supernatural Disappearances* (Robert Hale, 1995)

Eirik the Red and other Icelandic Sagas [trans. Gwyn Jones] (The World's Classics, Oxford University Press, 1961)

Forman, Joan, *The Mask of Time* (MacDonald and Jane's, 1978)

Graves, Robert, *The Greek Myths* (Penguin Classics, 1955)

Green, Celia, and McCreery, Charles, *Apparitions* (Hamish Hamilton, 1975)

Guizot, François, *History of the English Revolution* [trans. William Hazlitt] (H.G. Bohn, 1856)

Gurney, Edmund, Myers, Frederick W.H., and Podmore, Frank, *Phantasms of the Living* (1886)

Herodotus, *The Histories* [trans. Aubrey de Selincourt] (The Penguin Classics, 1955)

Holy Bible (Oxford University Press, 1876)

Hone, William, *The Every-Day Book* (Ward, Lock & Co., 1889)

Hone, William, *The Table Book*, vol. i (Hunt and Clarke, 1827)

Howell, James, *Epistolae Ho-Elianae: Familiar Letters* (Thomas Guy, 1672)

Ingpen, Roger (editor), *Shelley [Poems and prose]* (Herbert & Daniel)

James, Montague Rhodes, *The Apocryphal New Testament* (Oxford at the Clarendon Press, 1969)

Jones, Frederick L. (editor), *The Letters of Mary W. Shelley* (University of Oklahoma Press, 1946)

Lalanne, Ludovic, *Curiosités des Traditions des Moeurs et des Légendes* (Paulin, 1847)

Lang, Andrew, *Dreams and Ghosts* (Longmans, Green, and Co., 1899)

Light: A Journal of Psychical, Occult, and Mystical Research (Issues: 19 December 1885; 12 January, 2 February, 23 February 1889; 22 February 1890; 28 April 1894)

Doubles

MacKenzie, Donald, *Egyptian Myth and Legend* (Gresham Publishing Company)

Marchand, Leslie (editor), *Between Two Worlds, Byron's Letters and Journals*, vol. VII (John Murray)

Martin, Martin, *A Description of the Western Isles of Scotland* (Ambrose Bell, 1703)

Mysteries of the Unexplained (The Reader's Digest Association, 1988)

New Wonderful Magazine and Marvellous Chronicle, vol. III (1794)

Patterson, R.F. [editor], *Ben Jonson's Conversations with William Drummond* (Blackie and Son Limited, 1923)

Pliny, *Natural History* [translated by John Bostock and H.T. Riley] (Bohn's Library)

Salt, Henry S., *Percy Bysshe Shelley* (William Reeves, 1898)

Seltman, Charles, *Wine in the Ancient World* (Routledge & Kegan Paul, 1957)

Shirley, Ralph, *The Mystery of the Human Double* (The Olympia Press, 1972)

Stevenson, Rev. Joseph (trans.), *Church Historians of England*, vol. IV (Seeleys, 1856)

Strickland, Agnes, *Life of Queen Elizabeth* (Everyman Edition, 1906)

True Irish Ghost Stories [compiled by St John D. Seymour and Harry Neligan] (Humphrey Milford, 1926)

Twain, Mark, *Tom Sawyer, Detective, and Other Tales* (Chatto and Windus, 1897)

Underwood, Peter, *Haunted London* (Harrap, 1973)

Webb, J.F. (trans.), *Lives of the Saints* (Penguin Books, 1965)

Wright, C.E., *The Cultivation of Saga in Anglo-Saxon England* (Oliver and Boyd, 1936)

Index

Index

191